"I'm stayin

Juliette stood fro[...] her. "But…there'[...] already agreed to cooperate." A feeling of desperation rose that had nothing to do with their deal and everything to do with the feelings he stirred inside her. "You can't stay. I don't want you here."

Sam gave her a thin smile. "I trust you exactly as much as you trust me. That's to say, not at all. You and I are going to be joined at the hip for the duration of this assignment. Get used to it."

"This isn't acceptable." She hurried after him, protesting again as he ducked into her bedroom. "No, not that one…"

He turned around so suddenly that she ran into him. The heat from his hands on her shoulders seared into her. The hint of a drawl in his voice sent an involuntary shiver down her spine. "I'm in charge. You're in no position to bargain, or to make demands. The sooner you learn that, the better for both of us."

Dear Reader,

Our exciting month of May begins with another of bestselling author and reader favorite Fiona Brand's Australian Alpha heroes. In *Gabriel West: Still the One*, we learn that former agent Gabriel West and his ex-wife have spent their years apart wishing they were back together again. And their wish is about to come true, but only because Tyler needs protection from whoever is trying to kill her—and Gabriel is just the man for the job.

Marie Ferrarella's crossline continuity, THE MOM SQUAD, continues, and this month it's Intimate Moments' turn. In *The Baby Mission*, a pregnant special agent and her partner develop an interest in each other that extends beyond police matters. Kylie Brant goes on with THE TREMAINE TRADITION with *Entrapment*, in which wickedly handsome Sam Tremaine needs the heroine to use the less-than-savory parts of her past to help him capture an international criminal. Marilyn Tracy offers another story set on her Rancho Milagro, or Ranch of Miracles, with *At Close Range*, featuring a man scarred—inside and out—and the lovely rancher who can help heal him. And in Vickie Taylor's *The Last Honorable Man*, a mother-to-be seeks protection from the man she'd been taught to view as the enemy—and finds a brand-new life for herself and her child in the process. In addition, Brenda Harlan makes her debut with *McIver's Mission*, in which a beautiful attorney who's spent her life protecting families now finds that *she* is in danger—and the handsome man who's designated himself as her guardian poses the greatest threat of all.

Enjoy! And be sure to come back next month for more of the best romantic reading around, right here in Intimate Moments.

Leslie J. Wainger
Executive Senior Editor

Please address questions and book requests to:
Silhouette Reader Service
U.S.: 3010 Walden Ave., P.O. Box 1325, Buffalo, NY 14269
Canadian: P.O. Box 609, Fort Erie, Ont. L2A 5X3

Entrapment
KYLIE BRANT

Silhouette®

INTIMATE MOMENTS™

Published by Silhouette Books

America's Publisher of Contemporary Romance

SILHOUETTE BOOKS

ISBN 0-373-27291-X

ENTRAPMENT

Copyright © 2003 by Kim Bahnsen

All rights reserved. Except for use in any review, the reproduction
or utilization of this work in whole or in part in any form by any
electronic, mechanical or other means, now known or hereafter
invented, including xerography, photocopying and recording, or in
any information storage or retrieval system, is forbidden without
the written permission of the editorial office, Silhouette Books,
233 Broadway, New York, NY 10279 U.S.A.

All characters in this book have no existence outside the imagination of
the author and have no relation whatsoever to anyone bearing the same
name or names. They are not even distantly inspired by any individual
known or unknown to the author, and all incidents are pure invention.

This edition published by arrangement with Harlequin Books S.A.

® and TM are trademarks of Harlequin Books S.A., used under license.
Trademarks indicated with ® are registered in the United States Patent
and Trademark Office, the Canadian Trade Marks Office and in other
countries.

Visit Silhouette at www.eHarlequin.com

Printed in U.S.A.

Books by Kylie Brant

KYLIE BRANT

lives with her husband and children. Besides being a writer, this mother of five works full-time teaching learning disabled students. Much of her free time is spent in her role as professional spectator at her kids' sporting events.

An avid reader, Kylie enjoys stories of love, mystery and suspense—and she insists on happy endings! She claims she was inspired to write by all the wonderful authors she's read over the years. Now most weekends and all summer she can be found at the computer, spinning her own tales of romance and happily-ever-afters.

She invites readers to check out her online read in the reading room at eHarlequin.com. Readers can write to Kylie at P.O. Box 231, Charles City, IA 50616, or e-mail her at kyliebrant@hotmail.com. Her Web site address is www.kyliebrant.com.

For Jared—
who gets to be first, because being the oldest
has its privileges! I love you, honey.
Mom

Chapter 1

The lady was a thief.

Sam Tremaine watched the woman waltzing around the large ballroom, passing laughingly from one man's arms to another. Even among the glitz and glitter of the Parisian consulate party, she stood out in a way guaranteed to draw the men's eyes and the women's envy.

He stroked his index finger absently along the stem of the crystal flute in his hand, the expensive champagne forgotten for the moment. He wasn't surprised to find her at ease in the elegant social circle. He imagined she'd accepted the invitation he'd arranged on her behalf as her due. Beautiful, unattached women were sought after by hostesses looking to attract wealthy, powerful men to their parties. There would be no reason for any of the guests to see beyond her glamorous laughing surface. No reason to suspect that her beautiful, passionate face hid a soul as black as sin.

Her pictures hadn't done her justice. The errant thought occurred, and he considered it objectively. He had a file bulging with photos of her, taken by tele-photo lens when she was unaware. The flat two-di-mensional likenesses hadn't captured the energy that crackled around her, the incredible vivacity. In con-trast to the heap of pictures was pitifully little back-ground information. Juliette Morrow was shrouded in mystery. Most created identities were.

Sam set his half-full glass on a tray carried by a white-jacketed server and declined a replacement. He preferred to keep all his wits about him for the next step in this game. For it was a game; a contest in wits, bravado and cunning. And as in all games, it was one he intended to win.

He'd been watching her since she'd entered the room and he'd made certain she knew it. But far from the welcoming smile with which she graced her dance partners, she made a point of not looking in his direction too often. Perhaps she sensed a threat from him. If so, she had excellent instincts.

Purposefully, he began cutting through the dancing couples with deliberate strides. He noted the exact instant she saw him coming for her. That polite mask slipped a little, giving him a glimpse of…not fear. Wariness, maybe. And then her glance flicked away as if making note of the nearest exits.

"Excusez-moi. Est-ce que je puis emprunter cette belle dame?"

The portly balding man dancing with Juliette shrugged good-naturedly at his request and stepped back. Sam barely missed a beat before taking her in his arms and whirling her away. Because he was watching her so closely, he could see the struggle taking place in her expression, before she smoothed it with almost imperceptible effort.

"Monsieur Tremaine, the American lawyer. What brings you to our city?"

The flirtatious tone couldn't disguise the very real interest behind the question. He'd shaken her by his unswerving regard this evening, just as he'd intended. The quiet sense of satisfaction that filled him at the realization was derived as much from the personal as the professional. "You know my name. Should I be flattered?"

"I doubt it. You don't look like a man susceptible to flattery."

Sam almost smiled. Her observation was right on the mark. Instincts hummed to life as adrenaline spiked through him. Without a worthy opponent, even the most noble games lacked challenge.

"With you, I may make an exception." There was a painful twinge in his thigh, reminding him that the damaged muscle there hadn't completely healed. To take some of the strain off his leg, he adjusted his movements until they were barely swaying to the music. She followed him effortlessly, but he could feel the rigidity in her spine beneath his palm.

"I know your name, too. Juliette Morrow." He waited a beat before adding, "Or do you prefer the nickname the French press has for you? *Le petit voleur.* The little thief."

He watched her reaction to his words with interest. There was a flicker of something in her wide dark eyes, there and gone too quickly to be identified.

Then she tipped her head back and gurgled out an infectious laugh that had heads turning toward them.

"Do all Americans have such an offbeat sense of humor?" she inquired, once she'd recovered. There was real amusement in her voice. If he hadn't been so certain he was right, he might have doubted the conclusions he'd drawn. But he didn't doubt them. Which made her a liar, as well as a thief.

"I've been told I have a dry sense of humor, but I'm not joking now. And I think you know it. That's why your pulse is racing." He lifted her hand and pressed his lips to her pulse, felt it gallop beneath his touch.

"It isn't often I find myself in the arms of such an attractive man. What a pity to find that you're demented, as well." Her voice was cool, her gaze direct. "They say that mental illness is on the rise in your country. Perhaps in your line of work you find that quality an asset."

Despite himself, Sam grinned. Her English was flawless, as was her aim. "Lawyer jokes...the bond that unites cultures. I'm too used to them to take exception." Deliberately, he brushed his hand along the silky line of her back, left bare by her gown. He was gratified to feel her shiver in response, then used her reaction as an excuse to pull her closer.

She pressed both her hands against his chest, maintaining a small distance between them. "I've heard that Americans often romanticize criminals. Is your joke supposed to serve as some sort of compliment? A word of warning—few women find it flattering to be called thieves. If that's your idea of flirtation, you really need to get out more."

Sam didn't try to keep the smile from his lips. God

help him, but he was enjoying this. He didn't want to consider what that said about him. "You prefer flirtation of another sort, don't you? Flirting with danger, with the police." He lowered his head to the side of her throat, distracted for a moment by the scent that lingered there. "What do you enjoy most, I wonder?" He breathed the words in her ear, even as he filled his lungs with her perfume. "The research, the planning…or the actual theft? Does the prize ever really measure up to the anticipation? Does the risk-taking get in your blood, driving you to dare even more? A good psychiatrist would have a field day with those questions."

"A good psychiatrist is exactly what *you* need. I'll leave you to make an appointment." She pressed harder on his chest, attempting to free herself, but his arms only tightened.

"You'll find I'm a little more difficult to escape than the German police were last month." She didn't gasp at his words; she didn't seem to breathe at all. "The Riemenschneider was an exquisite pick, by the way. Intricate but balanced style, without the emotionalism of the period. But then I assume you had a buyer lined up before the job. A private collector?"

Juliette had given up the pretense of dancing, so Sam followed suit. His thigh screamed its appreciation.

Her voice, when it came, dripped disdain. "You'll have to excuse me. I have a low tolerance for boredom, and this conversation is growing tedious."

"Then let's go out to the balcony to continue our discussion. I'll take great care not to bore you, I promise." He exerted the slightest pressure with the palm of his hand against her back. She didn't move.

Looking around, she caught the eye of their host, Jean-Paul Rossiere. "I've tried civility, now I'll be blunt. Either you leave me alone, now, or I'll summon our host to have you removed." Rossiere was already making his way toward him, drawn, no doubt, by the manufactured look of entreaty in Juliette's big dark eyes.

"Good idea," Sam murmured imperturbably. He waved to the approaching Frenchman. "Jean-Paul might find this conversation interesting. His cousin is married to the CEO of International Safety Mutual, did you know that? Their insurance company has taken a beating at the hands of *le petit voleur* in recent years. I'm sure he'd be fascinated by what I have to say to you." He straightened as the Frenchman reached them, his watchful expression giving lie to the smile on his lips.

"Mademoiselle Morrow, are you enjoying yourself this evening?"

"As a matter of fact, Jean-Paul..." Sam started.

"Mr. Tremaine and I were just about to step outside for some fresh air." Juliette smiled brilliantly at Rossiere as she placed her hand on Sam's arm. "The party is lovely, but I'm afraid I'm in need of a rest before I begin another round of dancing."

The slight crease of worry eased from the other man's face. "Of course. It is becoming a bit stuffy in here, *n'est-il pas?* The balcony is just beyond those doors."

They moved in the direction he pointed, but Sam wasn't fooled by Juliette's seeming about-face. Her capitulation didn't signal defeat, but merely a change of venue for the next leg of the battle. He could appreciate her strategy even as he recognized its futility.

Drifting through the double French doors, Sam steered her past the couples lingering on the balcony toward a secluded area in the opposite corner. The night air was clear, fresh and keen as a blade. Shrugging out of his dinner jacket, he draped it around Juliette's bare shoulders, the chivalry of the action too ingrained to be considered.

She glanced up at him, still wary, her fingers clutching the jacket's lapels to keep it from sliding away. Turning to face her, he propped his hips against the ornate wrought-iron railing. Slipping an arm around her waist, he brought her close enough to stand between his spread legs, and left his arms looped loosely around her middle.

"If this was an elaborate scheme to get me outside alone, you get marks for creativity, at least."

He deliberately dashed the hint of relief in her statement with his next words. "We'll be assured privacy if people think we're infatuated with each other."

She strained away, as far as his grasp would allow. "And if you attempt to convince them of that, *you'll* be assured of an ambulance."

He was concentrating more on her voice than its content. "Where'd you grow up? I'm betting New York...Philadelphia. There's a slightly clipped quality to your speech that you haven't quite lost, despite the lovely French accent you've acquired."

She tipped her face up, gazed at him boldly. "Ah, now it becomes clearer. You've mistaken me for someone else. I'm almost disappointed." She reached out then, startling him, and cupped his jaw with slender fingers. The brisk air couldn't dissipate the warmth trailing in the touch. "Whoever she is, I'm not sure whether to envy or pity her."

When she would have taken her hand away, he raised his hand to cover hers. "Envy?"

"Unfortunately, it's not every day that a woman meets such a virile man. She could be forgiven for overlooking some of your less attractive qualities."

Their gazes clashed. The star-studded night sky turned her eyes into fathomless dark pools that invited a man to wade in and sink helplessly in their depths. She'd been beautiful inside, illuminated by the softened lights. In the moonlight she was stunning. Her dark hair was pulled on top of her head, leaving only the occasional errant curl free. It tempted a man to release it, to plunge his hands into the dark silky mass as it tumbled to her shoulders. Her dress was black, a glittery tube of material that showcased her curves and hinted at seductive promises.

She swayed closer. Again Sam caught the delicate scent she wore, something sexy and elusive. The pale porcelain of her skin shimmered in the darkness, inviting a caress, one long heated stroke. Hormones, operating on a different level from that of his brain, stood at alert.

Juliette raised her free hand, and his jacket clung to her shoulders for a moment, before sliding to the ground. She dipped her index finger in the shallow indentation in his chin that made shaving such a pain. "I have to admit wishing we'd met under different circumstances." When she went up on her tiptoes to press her lips against his, Sam recognized that the game had shifted. He was male enough to welcome the change.

He pulled her closer and sank into the taste of her. Her flavor imploded on his senses. Exotic. Forbidden. Exquisitely sensual. Her lips opened beneath his and his tongue swept in, found the darkly seductive taste stronger there. It went to his head faster than his favorite Scotch and was twice as lethal.

She gave a little gasp and went boneless, her body melding to his. For an instant he had a vision of what it would be like to have her naked, her body twisting beneath him. She'd be lightning in a man's arms, strobing heat and emotion. Making love to her would be like plunging into a chasm of wicked flames. Damned if he wasn't beginning to believe it'd be worth the fall.

Dragging his mouth from hers, he found himself distracted by the pulse beating wildly beneath her jaw. "Try the front one." He breathed the words into her ear before taking the lobe between his teeth.

"What?"

It pleased him that her voice wasn't quite steady. "Try my front pocket. My wallet's not in there either, but you might find something else of interest nearby."

He was prepared for her reaction, so he caught her fists in his hand before she could use them on him. Her struggles brought her hip into sharp contact with his injured thigh. He grunted, the now familiar pain lancing through him. He solved the problem by simply wrapping his arms around her and bringing her too tightly against him to wreak anymore damage. He hoped.

"Vous êtes fils d'une chienne!"

"Insulting my parentage isn't going to solve anything. What were you looking for, anyway? Not money, since I doubt you need it. ID?'' Her sharply hissed breath was its own answer. "As much as I was enjoying the search, I don't carry ID with me. You never know when a gorgeous woman will use her clever fingers to pick your pockets.''

Juliette glared at him, and he took a moment to appreciate the storm in her eyes. So he had only himself to blame when she stomped her stiletto heel sharply into his foot.

"Dammit!'' The resulting throb served as a vivid reminder of the seriousness of this encounter. He gave her a little shake. "Settle down. We're attracting attention.''

She obeyed, but her voice when it came was a dangerous purr. "You dare to call me a pickpocket? I could go to those gallery doors and have a dozen men rush to defend my honor for that insult alone.''

"Funny how the term pickpocket offends you more than 'thief.' I'll keep that in mind. But we both know that you aren't going to summon any of your admirers from in there.''

She tipped her head back defiantly. "Do we? And why is that?''

"Because I'm about to tell you everything I've found out about Juliette Morrow. It isn't much, all things considered. Given enough time, I'm sure I could discover more.'' And he wished, more than was comfortable, that he had that kind of time. Wished for answers to questions better not asked. Better not considered.

She yanked at her hands, and, because he thought her temper had passed, he released her. "If you had done near the research you claim, you would have learned that *le petit voleur* is a man, hence the name." Her shoulders straightened, as if daring him to disagree. "I think you'll agree that I am very much a female."

His mouth quirked. "I can certainly attest to the last statement, but the press's nickname is merely a reflection of perception, isn't it? Who would expect the most notorious thief on the continent to be a young woman?"

She gave him a pitying glance. "I am not sure what kind of women you are used to in America. In France, we understand that females are far different from males. We lack the strength, the daring necessary for the feats you accuse me of." Her hand went to her chest, one finger absently traced the bodice where material met bare skin. It was a maneuver meant to underscore her words, to draw attention to her femininity. "In my country, we accept those differences. We…embrace them." Her voice trailed off suggestively.

He was hard-pressed to know whether to kiss her or applaud. In the end, he did neither. "Bet those words were hard to say. But then, acting is part of your role, isn't it?" He knew by the heat in her gaze that he'd scored a direct hit. "It doesn't matter. We both know you don't mean them. You've been thumbing your nose at the rest of the world for so long I doubt you remember where the pretense ends and you really begin." There was a flash of expression on her face, there and gone too quickly to be identified. But he had the feeling that fleeting as it was, it was the first true response she'd shown him all evening.

"You know nothing about me."

Raising his brows, he said, "No? How about if I just run through my information and you can see for yourself?" He leaned back a little and let the railing behind him take some of the weight off his leg. "It's a convoluted little past you've concocted, and I have to hand it to you, damn hard to check out. Born at home outside Savigny...taken to live in Sweden when you were an infant...of course, before your birth could be recorded."

She reached up, smoothed a tendril of hair back from her face. "There wasn't time. My mother was very much in love with my father, and he wanted to take her back to his home country."

"So much in love with her that he didn't bother to marry her, but hey, I guess that would have left a paper trail, too, so you were wise to avoid that convention."

Her gaze narrowed. "Are you insulting my parents now?"

"You mean the way you did mine earlier? No. Just remarking on the convenience of the past you've spun for yourself. By the way, having your mother be an American living abroad was sheer brilliance. Allows you to establish dual citizenship, and that must come in handy."

"Well, I'm glad my life's story has provided you with such entertainment." Her words were glacial. "Perhaps you could get to the part where I need to steal for a living."

Sam folded his arms across his chest. Not even to himself would he admit it was to keep from reaching for her again. "You mean because you're an heiress, living off a modest trust you inherited upon your parents' early deaths? Again, a nice touch. And it does thwart those pesky questions of how you live without visible means of support."

"It hasn't seemed to thwart yours."

He shook his head. "I'm trained to look beneath the surface. To see what others have missed. Even a trail with as many twists and turns as yours can be followed, given the right incentive."

She stooped to pick up his jacket which had dropped earlier, and draped it again around her shoulders. He had no doubt she'd checked the pockets, surreptitiously, before she'd turned her attentions to him. "And your incentive would be…"

"I want to acquire your services."

This time she couldn't hide her reaction to his words. He took in her frozen expression with satisfaction. "We'll have to work out a different sort of arrangement than you're undoubtedly used to, but I think you'll find it to your benefit."

It didn't take her long to recover. "As…intriguing as that offer sounds, I'll have to refuse. I don't provide any services that are for sale."

The music started up again in the ballroom, and couples on the balcony began drifting back inside. "I'm not offering to hire you, actually. More like work out a trade."

"And here I thought you couldn't get more offensive," Juliette said coolly. "How unfortunate to be proven wrong." She slipped out of the jacket and laid it over his shoulder.

He watched her turn that slender bare back on him and start away. She got exactly three steps before he said, "Threats aren't really my style, but if you decline, the file I've accumulated on you could be turned over to the local authorities. I think you'd find it less inconvenient to cooperate than to be subjected to their questions."

"Do your worst, Mr. Tremaine." She looked back over her shoulder, her face serenely confident. "I've got absolutely nothing to hide."

He still hadn't adjusted to the time change. At least that was the reason Sam gave himself for being in the large well-equipped exercise room instead of upstairs asleep. He sank a blow into the body bag and danced away before it swayed his way again. Then, his actions a blur, he landed one blow after another, swift deadly jabs that would have rendered an opponent incapacitated.

"I hope the pounding that bag's taking isn't an indication of your frustration over this evening's events."

Sam didn't bother to turn around at the voice. He already knew who'd be standing there, and Miles Caladesh topped the list of the people he least felt like talking to right now. "I told you I'd report in the morning." With a studied movement he slammed his fist into the middle of the bag, sending it swaying.

"It *is* morning. I heard you as I came in and thought I'd get an update now."

He wasn't going away. Sam turned, resting a glove on top of the bag, and studied the other man. He didn't ask how Miles had spent the evening. He didn't need to. Too much alcohol had left his face flushed, and the fact that he'd returned to their borrowed quarters at all meant that his evening hadn't turned out as he'd hoped. A fact which renewed Sam's belief in the intelligence of the opposite sex.

"I made contact, as planned."

"And?"

"And…" Sam tapped his other gloved hand against his leg. "Nothing. Yet. She isn't going to just fold. She hasn't gotten this far by lacking guts." Honor, perhaps, but not guts. And to him, there could be nothing more damning.

"So we put the screws to her. If you'd listened to me you would have started out that way. When you're dealing with the dregs of society, you don't get anywhere by asking nicely. A show of force works quicker and is more effective in the long run."

"Really? I didn't realize you had any experience in the field, Miles. Is that what worked on your assignments?"

His words, delivered in a polite enough tone, had the man flushing even further. "I've pored over enough operation reports to know how things work."

"Paperwork?" Sam didn't bother to keep the derision from his voice. "There's a big difference between what gets put in the reports and the actual fieldwork. Maybe before your next promotion you'll realize that."

"I was just offering another possibility. Hotter than hell in here," the other man muttered. He reached up to loosen his tie.

"Step one is to initiate contact. That's been accomplished." Nothing would be gained by allowing his distaste for Caladesh to show, Sam thought. They were paired for the course of this operation, regardless of his wishes. And being the nephew of the United States president's wife gave Caladesh a certain standing, however undeserved.

Bringing one of his gloves to his mouth, Sam used his teeth to untie it. Shaking it off, he turned his attention to unlacing the other. "Whatever your opinion of Morrow, rushing things isn't the answer."

"So you think she's going to come to her senses and cooperate?"

Sam's lips curved a little as he thought of the defiant look Juliette had tossed him, the dismissive disdain in her voice. "Not willingly." She'd called his bluff, and he couldn't blame her. He'd have done the same thing in her position. And since there was no chance in hell of him giving his file to the French authorities, or anyone else, it was a safe enough move.

"Not…" Miles stared at him, then jammed his hand through his meticulously groomed brown hair. "Need I remind you what we have riding on this operation?"

Sam walked over to the weight bench and adjusted it for leg lifts, then sat down. He certainly didn't need any reminders. The memory of Sterling, his previous case officer, still burned. It had only recently been discovered that the CO had been a mole working for the very man Sam had spent the better part of two years investigating. One agent had already been killed, and sheer luck was the only thing that had saved Sam from the same fate once Sterling had revealed Sam's last assignment. With the former CO on the run, it was impossible to know just how badly the agency had been compromised. Which explained the change of rules on this mission.

He positioned one foot beneath the bar, gritted his teeth and lifted. The muscles in his injured thigh screamed a protest. Ignoring the pain, he gulped in a breath and concentrated on counting the lifts. This investigation was too critical to national security to not move forward, but they were utilizing an unusual degree of inner agency secrecy. Sam reported to Miles, and Miles reported directly to Headquarters. The taint of corruption negated the usual chain of command, and their tactics had shifted accordingly.

Belatedly, Sam realized Caladesh was waiting for a response. "She didn't respond to the threat I made tonight…she's too smart for that. So we'll move on to step two."

The other man watched him for a moment, silent. Then he said, "How long before you get her cooperation?"

"Not long." Despite the fact that his file on Juliette Morrow elicited more questions than answers, he'd come to know her on some level, long before they'd actually met. He'd begun to understand a little about how her mind worked. And become fascinated in the process. "She just needs more convincing, that's all."

"I guess I'll have to assume you know what the hell you're doing here," Miles said, his voice doubtful. "At least Headquarters seems to believe you do. I'm going to allow you a little latitude on this assignment, Tremaine, but only a little. If Morrow slips through our fingers, this assignment is badly compromised."

The weights descended to their resting place with a clatter. The muscles in Sam's leg were shuddering with strain. Tersely he retorted, "I don't need your reminders of what's at stake here. It was my agent who was tortured and killed, remember?"

When the man turned and strode stiffly from the room, Sam cursed, long and inventively. He was capable of diplomacy, so there was really no reason for him to antagonize the man, despite his opinion of him. Miles's presence here was an irritant, but it wasn't contributing to Sam's insomnia.

No, the cause of that could be traced to Juliette Morrow. He readjusted the bench for some overhead presses, a deep frown creasing his forehead. She fit into his investigation in a way he never would have predicted, and right now offered them their best opportunity to strike at their target. He'd discovered what she ate, what she wore, where she went, who she spoke to. Those details had been compiled with a painstaking precision that was no more or less meticulous than every other assignment he'd worked.

And that's all this was. An assignment. Morrow represented a means to an end, and he'd use her in the mission with the same clinical detachment he employed with any other contacts he recruited.

Lowering the bar and weights slowly to his chest, Sam pumped it upward again. The repetitive motion should have soothed, but only proved to be a strenuous metronome to his thoughts. His greatest strength as an agent lay in the fact that he didn't grow confused by the shadowy areas his job strayed into. Honor was more than a code to him; it was a way of life. It allowed him to see black and whites where other agents saw murky shades of gray. Involving Juliette Morrow in this assignment wasn't going to change that.

It wouldn't be allowed to.

Chapter 2

Juliette entered her home with all the stealth of the thief Sam Tremaine had accused her of being. It wasn't until she'd closed her bedroom door behind her that she let her temper flare. She snatched the hairbrush from her dressing table and hurled it toward her bed.

Damnez-l'à l'enfer! Damn damn damn him to hell!

Her comb went the way of the brush, followed by a carved teak pin box and an antique pill bottle. Breathing heavily, she fisted her hands at her sides. If Tremaine had been standing in front of her, she'd have taken great satisfaction in landing a sucker punch right on his sexily dented chin.

She whirled toward the dressing table to search for another missile and stopped short when she saw the figure standing in her bedroom doorway.

"Well, darling, it's been a while since I've seen

you throw a tantrum like that.'' Pauline Fontaine strolled casually into the room, wearing an elegant dressing gown. Even at eighty, her posture was straight, her movements graceful. Age, Pauline was fond of saying, couldn't negate breeding. "Don't tell me Lockhart beat you to that Monet you had your eye on?"

"No, of course not. Lockhart lacks the imagination and the cunning. I'm sorry, Grandmama.'' Guilt pushed temper aside as Juliette went to her grandmother. "I didn't mean to wake you."

"You didn't, child. I wasn't asleep, and thought I'd check to see if you'd returned yet. And you have, obviously." A smile tugged at the older woman's lips. "Mind telling me what, or who, has gotten you in such a snit?"

"I'm not in a snit, I'm seriously pissed off." Juliette gave her grandmother a hug and ignored her sound of dismay at her choice of words. "I met a man tonight, and…" She stopped, and moved away from the older woman while she decided how much to tell her. Her grandmother's advanced years had weakened her heart, if not her iron will. There was no use burdening her with details that she would only fret over.

"A man?" By her delighted tone, it was plain that Pauline had been successfully distracted. "Tell me about him. He must be unique, indeed, to have drawn this level of emotion from my cool, collected granddaughter."

"Unique?" Juliette gave a short laugh, and turned to pace. "You could say that. There's certainly nothing ordinary about Sam Tremaine." He'd caught her attention the moment he'd made his entrance. Other

women this evening had sent not-so-subtle admiring
gazes his way, drawn no doubt by his bright shock
of short blond hair, that angular poet's face, his
wicked green eyes. But it hadn't been his looks that
had elicited her immediate instinctive reaction. It had
been the danger he'd radiated.

It would have been hard to miss. He projected an
aura of power, partially glossed beneath a suave
handsome presence, but there, nonetheless. The elegant black tux should have contained the shimmer of
menace that surrounded him, but had only showcased
it. She'd spent the evening hoping that the threat she
sensed from him was purely masculine. Discovering
otherwise was as much a slap at her femininity as it
was to her safety.

"So. Tell me more about this not-ordinary-at-all
man."

Startled, Juliette looked back over her shoulder.
She'd almost forgotten her grandmother's presence
in the room. "He's an American. A lawyer, he
says." Aware of the agitation in her movements, she
slowed, walked to the bed to retrieve the things she'd
thrown.

"You say that as though you don't believe it."

"I believe he's more." Crossing to the dressing
table, she replaced the items neatly on its surface.
She looked in the mirror to see her grandmother had
followed her, and their gazes met. "He might pose
a small problem for us."

"What kind of problem?"

"He seems to think he has discovered *le petit voleur's* identity."

Pauline said nothing for a moment. Then she
sighed. "Ah."

"He has nothing but supposition to go on, of course." She was banking a great deal on that. But she didn't need to tell her grandmother how serious it would be if even a breath of his suspicion made its way to the local police.

"Does he represent law enforcement? Insurance?"

Juliette reached up and began taking the pins from her hair. She always thought best when her hands were occupied. "I'm not sure." She wasn't in the mood to mention that her attempt to answer that question for herself had met with failure. The memory still stung. "I don't think so. He offered me a job."

"You don't think Jacques might have sent him to you?"

She shook her head, and the hair she'd released tumbled past her shoulders. "Jacques would have informed me beforehand. And Tremaine didn't reach that conclusion about my identity based on anything Jacques would have told him." Dropping the last of the pins on the dresser, she pushed her hands into her hair, shook it out. "At any rate, I think it would be best to remain inactive for a while. At least until I can gather some more information on Tremaine and what he's trying to accomplish."

"That's not acceptable. We can't afford to deviate from our time line." Pauline's voice was implacable, as it always was when this subject was discussed. "One doesn't duck in the face of obstacles, one finds a way around them."

Her vehemence drew a half smile from her granddaughter. "You're not fighting the Resistance anymore, Grandmama. A slight delay in any step of our plan isn't a matter of life or death."

Her teasing failed to soften the woman's attitude. Steely-eyed she retorted, "No, but it is a matter of honor. I know I don't have to remind you of that."

The words raked at old wounds, renewed their throb. No, she didn't need her grandmother's words to remember. The specters that haunted her dreams were reminder enough. Taking a deep breath, she dodged the emotions that threatened to surface and reached for logic. Part of the woman's adamance came from a fear she'd never live to see fruition of the goal they'd worked toward for so long. But analyzing the risks of each job was Juliette's job. It wouldn't do to become careless now.

"I can't stick too closely to our schedule. I don't know how much information he has on my activities." Just hearing the words out loud was infuriating. She'd come much too far to allow a mere man to interfere with her plans. And there was more than a little ego at stake, as well. If Sam Tremaine thought he could rattle her so easily, he hadn't discovered as much about her as he'd claimed.

A tiny smile crossed her lips as a strategy began to form in her mind. She'd spent the past decade learning how to create illusions. The game plan this time called for nothing more sophisticated than the old bait-and-switch. And when *le petit voleur* struck elsewhere while Juliette was still in Paris, Tremaine would be forced to admit he'd been wrong about her.

The prospect was delicious.

The slim steel cable glinted in the shadows of the darkened exhibit room in Copenhagen's famed Gallery of Art. The floor's guard had passed by two minutes earlier. If he stuck to his schedule he wouldn't be back for another eight minutes. The display case in the middle of the room would be empty in six.

The black-clad figure set the vent cover aside silently and snapped the buckle from the cable to the body harness. With quick movements, the body crawled to the edge of the vent and poised on the edge, hand outstretched.

The red light on the palm-size remote winked rapidly as it was aimed at first one security camera, then the other. Within seconds the cameras' power lights faded. The remote was clipped back on a belt, and with a quick tug, the strength of the cable was tested. A tiny whir was heard as the pulley mechanism activated and the figure was carried, legs curled upward, toward the center of the ceiling.

The red laser beams of the security system crisscrossed the space below in a random patchwork pattern. With the room rigged to be heat sensitive as well, it was thought by most to be impenetrable. They would soon be proven wrong. Every system was vulnerable. It was just a matter of research and ingenuity.

The Mylar suit the figure wore was stifling. It would successfully retain the body temperature, emitting a steady sixty degrees that wouldn't trip the alarms. Form-fitting, it allowed for maximum flexibility, a necessity for this job.

The body bowed and twisted to avoid the slim beams. As one was evaded, another loomed. The technique was reminiscent of a strange ballet, fluid streams of movement, flexible arching and seemingly impossible contortions. Until finally, the body hung upside down, suspended between two beams, within arm's reach of the glass case in the center of the room. The position would have to be held nearly motionless for the entire operation, taxing both muscles and nerves. If something was going to go wrong, it would likely be now.

A suction cup was taken from a pouch at the waist and affixed to the glass top. Next a vial was extracted, and dark gray powder shaken out in an outline atop the case, roughly the size of a basketball. That accomplished, one deep breath could be taken, but only one. There was far more to be done.

The first vial was exchanged for another. The cap was carefully removed and tucked away. Acid was poured with excruciating care. It raced around the circle, devouring the tiny grains with rapid greed. In the process the glass would be weakened, while the chemical reaction with the ingredients in the powder would deactivate any alarm on the market.

A cramp stabbed viciously, a blade between the ribs. A quick glance at an illuminated wrist watch showed five minutes remaining. So far so good. A slim glass cutter was taken from the pouch. The figure shifted a fraction. Both arms would be needed now. One was positioned with teeth-gritting caution between two red beams to grasp the knob on the suction cup. The other slid beneath a laser beam closer to the case. The cutter traced easily around the weakened circle in the glass, loosening it to be lifted and placed aside.

Anticipation thrummed. Time suspended. In the near darkness, everything else faded to insignificance. This was the moment that never failed to thrill. With near awe, a hand was slipped into the

opening, carefully freeing the necklace from its bed
of black velvet.

The perfectly matched pearls shimmered like
moon glow in the shadows, but it was the square-cut
twenty-carat ruby hanging from the center that commanded attention. With hypnotizing brilliance it
speared the darkness with shards of crimson. The
Moonfire necklace. In the past five centuries, count-
less women had coveted it. An untold number of
lives had been sacrificed for it. And now one man
would be denied it.

That knowledge brought the greatest satisfaction
of all.

Unhurriedly, the necklace was tucked away into
the pouch. The cramping pain increased, and a feeling of urgency rose. Two minutes left.

A moment was taken, and then another. Then with
slow, methodical movements, the black-clad body
was unbent, twisted, sinuous grace and fierce concentration evident as the pulley was reactivated, inch
by excruciating inch. It wasn't until the figure was
curled up against the cable that another deep breath
was taken.

Forty-five seconds.

With a near silent hum, the mechanism carried its
burden across the ceiling to the cold-air vent. As the
hole grew closer, a feeling of relief was allowed. The
whole operation would take less than the allotted six
minutes. By the time the guard noted what had tran-
spired, escape would already be well underway.

Thirty seconds.

The vent opening was within reach. The taste of
impending success was sweet. A feeling of unnatural
calm settled over the adrenaline. Hands braced

against the wall on either side of the opening, muscles bunched.

And then a light snapped on in the hallway outside the room, spotlighting the figure, freezing it in shock and dismay.

"Impressive." A slow solitary clapping accompanied the admiring statement. "I wouldn't have believed it if I hadn't seen it for myself. You're every bit as good as I've been led to believe."

The words, their meaning, didn't register. The man's presence did. The figure dove forward in one streak of motion, entering the narrow vent like an arrow fired from a crossbow. Panic licked at nerve endings, was beaten back. Cool logic was called on now. Near misses had happened before. They'd been infrequent, long, long ago, but they had occurred. Precautions were always taken. Alternate escape routes planned.

But never had this eventuality been considered.

There would be time later for second-guessing and self-recriminations. With the ease of long practice, everything but the primary goal was pushed aside. Escape.

The ventilation system was narrow. Movement was accomplished by wiggling forward while pushing off with the toes. Thirty feet ahead the pipes branched off into a maze of joints and tubes traveling to opposite corners of the gallery. When the time came, the figure bent an elbow, squeezed to the left. Another several feet, and a palm went up, felt along the top of the tubing for the hole that had been cut to allow entry.

At that point a body could stand, head and torso through the hole, a sense of freedom that should have relieved. But there was no time for relief. Once free of the ventilation pipe the figure could run, stooped but surprisingly rapid, along the crisscrossing tubing, moving from memory alone. Two rights then a left and a flying leap to the wall ladder. A speedy ascent and then a shoulder applied to the utility door with enough force that the figure stumbled out onto the gallery roof. The night sky had never looked so welcoming.

There was no time to enjoy it. It was one hundred yards to the edge of the roof. The time spent crossing it seemed interminable, but the thought of escape gave impetus. A cable was waiting on the east side, allowing descent to the alley between the gallery and the neighboring building. With the cable grasped in two hands, a body could rappel down the side of the building like a spider leaving its web.

The edge was reached. The figure leaned over, reached for the cable.

And found it missing.

"Looking for this?"

That dreaded voice came again, unbearably smug. Unbearably amused. Whirling, the black-clad figure faced the man, similarly dressed, who was already nearer than expected. The cable—that precious symbol of freedom—was looped around his wrist.

With his free hand, the man reached up, swept the black watch cap off his head. The moonlight painted his hair golden. And his eyes, those damned wicked green eyes, gleamed. "*Le petit voleur.* We meet again." Carelessly he stuck the cap in his back pocket and approached. A slow, single-minded stalking that was meant to hypnotize or to panic. The figure did neither.

"Weren't expecting company down there, huh?" Sam's voice was conversational. "I'm not surprised. You work alone, right? And you don't make mistakes often." He'd halved the distance between them with deliberate steps. Anticipation grew, was barely reined in. "The only one you made this time was in underestimating me."

Behind the mask, the figure smiled, a grim stretch of the lips. There had been an underestimation, all right. But Sam Tremaine was the one who'd made it.

He took a step closer. Another. And then he smiled. Slow and wide and devastating. "Whatever you're thinking, forget it. We're partners now. In case you haven't noticed, your options have just decreased dramatically." He stretched one gloved hand across the distance spanning them.

In a blur of motion a kick was aimed at his weakened thigh, a solid blow landed. Sam's leg buckled and he cursed, but he didn't go down completely, and he didn't loosen his grasp on the cable. The figure ran several feet past him, then turned and sprinted by him again, flying through the air even as his shout sounded. "Dammit, no!"

There was a moment of euphoria, as air whipped by, then a second of fear as the roof of the next building failed to materialize as rapidly as anticipated. Arms were outstretched, fingers flexed. When contact was made, the body scrabbled wildly, grasping for purchase, and settled on the narrow ledge edging the rooftop. It took every ounce of energy to pull up, to throw first one leg over the ledge, and then the other. Once safely on the roof, a lightning pace was set toward the other side. There was a fire escape fairly close beneath. From there, it was just a matter of…

It was like being hit from behind by a Mack truck. The figure went down hard, rolled, a huge weight attached. Vision was blurred by a dizzying array of stars. Lungs squeezed of oxygen. Helplessly, the figure lay there, trapped beneath Sam Tremaine's hard body, capable only of the fight for breath.

He recovered first. "Sonofbitch." His voice was grim. "You damned near killed us both."

Air resupplied oxygen, and with it came instinct. One leg was drawn up sharply, but he shifted, removing its intended target from range. "I'd just as soon you didn't finish me off right yet. I've got plans for you, little thief. But before I get into them…" He reached out, pushed the black hood slowly up to reveal features that would be all too familiar to him.

"Juliette." His gaze raked her form. "Your getup gives a whole new meaning to basic black."

"Bastard."

He caught her curled fist just before it clipped him neatly on the jaw. Drawing both of her wrists up above her head, he held them there with one hand. "It's a little early in our relationship for endearments. But if it weren't…" His teeth flashed. "I'd tell you that you look exquisite in moonlight."

She seethed, bucking beneath him. "Get off me."

Still grinning, he didn't move a muscle. "Your accent tends to fade when you're mad, did you know that?"

With effort, she stopped struggling. Despite her long-standing aversion to being held against her will, it was preferable to the indignity of being unable to move him an inch.

Dark gaze battled with green. Slowly the smile faded from his lips. For the first time she became aware of their isolation. It had to be close to two o'clock in the morning. Unlike New York, with its unending traffic and sounds of life, Copenhagen slept, at least in this business neighborhood.

Smokey tufts of black clouds bumped and shifted across the dark sky. Juliette had always felt at one with the night. Darkness was her accomplice. But tonight that relationship had been marred by Tremaine's appearance, and she wondered bleakly if things would ever be the same again.

The silence around them grew thick and fraught with tension. Her senses were always heightened on a job. Surely that explained why she was so aware of the weight of him, the heat. Her legs were caught between the hard length of his, the position much too intimate. Hips to hips. Breast to breast. Even their breath mingled. She moistened her lips, saw his gaze track the action and felt a thrill flicker through her at the desire in his eyes.

Juliette let her eyelids flutter, felt her stomach do the same. "Now that you've caught me, Sam, what are you going to do with me?"

Her question hung heavy in the night, the answer all too apparent in his expression. She'd seen passion on a man's face often enough to identify it. His gaze was arrowed on her mouth, and the hard curve of his own drew closer. Despite the insulated suit she wore, it would be difficult to miss the signs of his growing arousal. The stillness around them hummed with chemistry and it became increasingly difficult for her to breathe.

His eyes slitted. "First," he murmured, his voice raspy, "I'm going to relieve you of this."

Before his words even registered, his touch did. He shifted, one hand going to the pouch at her waist. She tried to jerk away, but she was still caught securely beneath him. The necklace glittered as it dangled from his grasp.

He gave a low tuneless whistle. "Nice." With a deft movement, he shoved it inside his shirt. "Not sure if it's worth the price you're going to pay, but I'll let you be the judge of that."

Her gaze narrowed. Given his careless tone, she would almost think she'd imagined the moments earlier. And if there wasn't physical evidence to the contrary, perhaps she would. But they were pressed too closely together for him to hide it.

From bitter experience Juliette knew the importance of controlling emotions. With that kind of control came power. Others could be manipulated through their feelings if one was able to remain detached. She understood that concept, embraced it.

So it shouldn't have been so infuriating that Sam Tremaine was obviously capable of the same.

Her tone belittling, she said, "And you call me a thief."

"Honey, you *are* a thief. And from what I witnessed tonight, a damn good one." When she tried to pull her wrists free from his grip, he tightened his hold. "Easy to see how you've escaped capture for so long. That little double you had standing in for you in Paris was sheer genius."

Since it was useless to deny it, she merely angled her jaw. "Not genius enough to fool you, apparently."

He gave a modest shrug. "You've been under surveillance for months, Juliette." When he saw her eyes widen he said, "Does that surprise you? I have more pictures of you than your own mother probably does. Videos of you walking. Shopping. Eating. Flirting." His voice got lower, grew almost caressing. "I know the way you move. The way you tilt that little chin of yours when you're telling someone to go to hell." His index finger tapped her chin, and she flinched. She felt like she was being stripped bare by his words, his revelations leaving her exposed and vulnerable. If he were telling the truth, how could she have not known it? Been aware of it?

And because she felt threatened, she lashed out. "Sounds perverted, Tremaine. If your pastime is stalking women, you need to find a new hobby."

"Not women, Juliette. Just you." The single syllable of his last word reverberated between them. "It wasn't enough to learn your identity. To track you down. I had to learn to think the way you do."

Of all the things he'd said so far, this was by far the most insulting. "Now you're telling me you know how my mind works?"

"I'm beginning to, I think. You've got nerves of steel. You'd have to. It was possible that you'd wait me out after I approached you at the consulate party. Very possible you'd engage in a game of wits with me. So the woman who looks so very like you in your penthouse, the one who never strays too close to any of the windows, could be mistaken for you."

Stubbornly she remained silent. Dammit, it should have worked. Had, more than once. "You followed me." The realization burned. There was no way he could have known her target. She'd deviated from the schedule, so even if he'd been privy to it, he couldn't have predicted her intention.

He shifted his weight a little, allowing her to breathe more easily. "I was counting on the probability that the most notorious thief on the continent would have a healthy ego. Why be kept inactive when you could make a fool out of me and continue your work, right?" Because there was enough truth in his words to sting, she refused to answer. It didn't seem to bother him. "You made a fairly convincing teenage boy. I never would have believed it if I hadn't seen it for myself."

"You couldn't have watched all the exits yourself." He didn't answer, and her stomach went queasy. How many people did Tremaine have working with him? And how was this going to impact her own plans, years in the making?

The inner questions stilled as he rose, pulling her to her feet. "We've wasted enough time. C'mon." While her wrists were still gripped in his hand, he used the other to divest her of the pouch at her waist. "We can continue this discussion on the way back to Paris. As a matter of fact, there's quite a bit we have to discuss."

His arrogance was astounding. "Even supposing you could actually manage to hang on to me while we get off the roof and make our way back to Paris, what makes you think I'll be any more cooperative now than before? No one else saw me in that gallery. You have the necklace, not me." A tiny smile began to play around her mouth. "I think you overplayed your hand here, Tremaine."

He took a step closer to her and she shivered involuntarily. Gone was the handsome charmer. His gaze was flat, his face hard. All that remained was the air of danger she'd sensed the first time she'd seen him.

"Don't make the mistake of thinking this is a game, Juliette. Once we're back in Paris you're going to do exactly what I tell you."

She gave an incredulous laugh. "If you believe that, you didn't research me nearly well enough. What makes you believe I'd ever agree to cooperate with you?"

He grasped her elbow and began guiding her toward the fire escape. "Because if you don't, I'll see to it that your grandmother spends the rest of her life in prison, in a cell right next to yours."

Chapter 3

Sam watched Juliette stalk from room to room in her luxurious Paris penthouse like a sleek feline on the prowl. And when she slammed the door of the last empty room and strode toward him, he braced himself in case she pounced.

"Where is she, Tremaine?"

He didn't make the mistake of underestimating the danger in her lethal purr. Not when it was coupled by that gleam in her eye. Nor did he pretend to misunderstand her.

"Your grandmother is safe with some associates of mine."

Juliette placed her balled-up fists on her hips, he assumed in an effort to restrain from using them on him. "I want to see her. Now."

Sam shook his head. He'd been up for two days. The sun had risen hours ago, and it would be several more hours before he'd get any sleep. During the near silent train ride back to Paris his leg had stiffened up on him, and right now his thigh was a twisting mass of cramping muscle. Pain tended to piss him off, and she was the cause of that pain, so he wasn't in the mood to be diplomatic. What he *was* in the mood for was a stiff Scotch and an hour in a whirlpool. Since he was unlikely to get either any time soon, there would be no concessions granted.

Juliette's first demand was quickly followed by another. "Then I want to talk to her."

"You and I have to come to terms first."

"Let me guess. You're thinking that you get to set those terms."

He allowed himself a grim smile. "Well, I am the one holding all the cards here, aren't I, honey?" Brushing by her, he went to the phone he spotted on the eighteenth-century desk near the window. Picking up the receiver, he dialed room service and ordered a pint of their finest Scotch, and then belatedly sent her an inquiring look. "Do you want breakfast?"

"No."

He turned back to the phone. "And send up two orders of eggs Benedict, a couple sides of potatoes and assorted pastries." Replacing the receiver, he turned back to her. "What you don't eat, I will."

She looked as if she were going to explode before she turned her back on him, visibly fighting for control. The close-fitting suit she'd worn earlier had been shed, along with the hood she'd used to cover her features. The black tank top she wore followed her curves faithfully and the snug-fitting black pants showcased the long line of her slender legs. Given the picture she made with her riot of long black curls and creamy skin, he imagined there were few men alive who wouldn't willingly give up some valuables in return for her company.

Of course, he reminded himself, she didn't make those kinds of trades. She took what she wanted, without regard to anyone's wishes. Consequences were variables to be weighed only as they affected her risk assessments. People unfortunate enough to be chosen as targets were given no consideration at all.

For a man who'd lived his life adhering to a cherished family code, her choices were reason enough to despise her.

She was moving about the penthouse with a smooth easy grace at odds with the steel in her spine. She'd picked up an ivory carving and held it in her palm, rubbing her fingers over it rhythmically.

He sat down on the overstuffed sofa, propped his feet on the matching hassock in front of him and barely managed to stifle a sigh of relief. The furniture was designed for both style and comfort. As a matter of fact, there'd been no expense spared in decorating the entire suite. Her career had been, to this point, quite lucrative.

"I have money."

Her bald statement could have been plucked from his thoughts. Rubbing his thigh with one hand, he cocked a brow at her. "I'm not surprised."

"I mean I can pay you. A reasonable price, at least." Apparently having reached a decision, she crossed toward him, her face stamped with determination. "All you have to do is release my grandmother. And turn over this file you claim to have."

He waited until she stood next to him before saying, "No." Taking her hand, he pulled her down next to him. He'd have to be dead from the neck down not to appreciate the way her dark eyes flashed. He was tired, not dead. "There's only one way for you to get your grandmother released."

"And that is?"

"To do exactly as I tell you." He could have been more persuasive, he could have been smoother. But where charm could be misconstrued as weakness, he knew she'd understand control. She was too used to wielding it herself to mistake it. And the sooner she learned that she was no longer calling the shots, the sooner the operation could commence.

She tugged at her hand. He didn't release it. "Tell me what you want."

It was, he knew, a concession of sorts. The first step toward admitting her options had narrowed dramatically. "I need something that someone else has."

"And you want me to steal it for you," she said flatly.

He inclined his head. "You have to admit that you're uniquely qualified. This job will be challenging, and secrecy is imperative. There are maybe ten people in the world capable of pulling it off. Three of them are in prison. *Le petit voleur* is one of the five top remaining candidates."

If his assessment of her ranking annoyed her, she didn't let it show. "If any of the five would have done as well, why go to the trouble of tracking my identity?"

"Because my target is Hans Oppenheimer."

Her face remained expressionless, her gaze steady on his. "Again…why me?"

He felt a flicker of admiration. She was a cool one, he'd give her that. "How do you think I discovered your identity, Juliette? It was Oppenheimer I was interested in all along. He's suspected of insurance fraud, did you know that?" Sam thought he saw a gleam of satisfaction in her eyes, there and gone so quickly he couldn't be sure he'd seen it at all. "He's sustained so many losses over the last several years that I'm told his insurance premiums are astronomical. He had to buy an insurance company himself because no one else would underwrite him."

"Life can be tragic for the rich."

"Can't it, though? Especially when you've been targeting him almost exclusively for the last five years. That's what led me to you. Law enforcement focuses on the individual thefts, or a pattern of them. That line of inquiry gets murky quickly, especially since they can't be sure which jobs to credit *le petit voleur* with, and which are the work of others. But my focus was Oppenheimer. He's a man who collects enemies. If he wasn't running an insurance scam, and was suffering real losses, that meant someone had singled him out. I followed that possibility and it led me to you."

She succeeded in pulling her hand away from him and with a studied movement shifted away, curling her feet under her. "Did he send you after me?"

Now it was his turn to be offended. "No, although I understand he's given several investigators that particular assignment. He seems to believe that a ring of thieves is responsible, hired by one of his rivals to deplete his resources."

She gave a little smile. "He sounds like a fool."

"Don't make the mistake of underestimating him.

The price he has on your head is one million American dollars.''

Cocking her head, she seemed to consider his words. "So he raised the reward. It's still rather low, given the value of everything he's lost, but he always was a man to want something for nothing."

There was a tinge of bitterness in her tone. He wondered what Oppenheimer had done to cause it. Sam knew exactly just what the man was capable of. "You sound like you know him well."

The words, quietly spoken, had her expression turning cautious. "You're not the only one who does research. So you're not representing Oppenheimer and your methods are too unorthodox for me to believe that you work for an insurance agency..." Her words trailed off as she raised her brows questioningly. When Sam didn't respond, she asked, "Exactly who are you working for?"

There was that flash of admiration again. He really was going to have to curb it, given the circumstances. But her instincts were, once again, right on the mark. "What makes you think I'm working for anyone? Maybe Oppenheimer has something of mine that I want back."

She was shaking her head before he even finished the words. "You've expended too much time, effort and manpower for that to be true. That translates into money. Lots of it. You may be independently wealthy, but most people with a grudge wouldn't go to these lengths to strike at their enemy."

"The details don't matter, my goal does. If that requires unorthodox methods, unorthodox allies..." He shrugged. "It's the end result I'm interested in." That much, at least was true. With the renewed interest in antiterrorist activities, executive orders had changed to allow for more latitude. An agent was no longer prohibited from recruiting criminals to further the country's goals.

Which only meant that now he could do so openly.

The discreet door buzzer sounded. "Must be room service. Check for sure before you let them in." If he tried to get up again, he was afraid his damn leg would give out on him completely. And he knew enough not to expose that kind of weakness to the woman beside him.

Woodenly, Juliette obeyed. She crossed to the door and looked out the peephole, saw the white-jacketed waiter in the hallway. She got some bills from her purse, opened the door and exchanged the tip for the food-laden tray.

"Put it here." He patted the cushion beside him, and she did as he bid. He studied the label on the Scotch with satisfaction. The French knew their liquor. Handing the bottle to Juliette, he asked this time, politely, he thought, "Can you pour me three fingers over ice?"

The civil phrasing of the request was obviously lost on her. She fairly snatched the bottle from his hand as she turned and marched to the galley kitchen. When she returned, he already had a plate balanced on his lap. He took the glass she thrust toward him and indicated the other plate. "You should eat something."

"I don't think so. There's something about blackmail that affects my appetite."

He considered her words as he tipped the glass to his lips. That first scalding slide of Scotch burned a path down his throat and pooled warmly in his belly.

The second dimmed the throbbing in his thigh, just a fraction. "Blackmail? That's an ugly word for a mutually beneficial business arrangement."

She gave a sharp laugh. "Is that what it's called these days? You kidnap my grandmother—yes," she stabbed a finger toward him when he opened his mouth to protest. "You can't pretty it up. You threaten her well-being in exchange for my cooperation. Not to mention the fact that you still have something that belongs to me."

That last statement had him choking on his first forkful of eggs. "If you're talking about the necklace, need I remind you that you *stole* it?"

"That's right, *I* stole it. I did the research, paid the expenses, figured the risks. Do you have any idea of the hours of practice I put in on that job?"

Color had risen in her cheeks. Sam watched her as he bit into a piece of bacon. Chauvinistically, he decided she was a woman who looked good with a storm in her eyes. He was intelligent enough not to tell her so. "I could see that. As a matter of fact, I've never watched anything like it." There had been something sensuous about the graceful contortions she'd undergone to dodge the laser beams. Just the memory was enough to heat his system much the way the Scotch had.

Deliberately, he pushed the mental picture aside. "It's that kind of attention to detail that we'll need on this effort."

She was silent for a moment, contemplating the ivory piece she'd set down on a nearby Chippendale table. Even from this distance he could tell the figure was quite old, a carving of some sort of pagan god. He wondered if it meant something special to her. It was useless to consider. It had nothing to do with his assignment. But after months of putting this job together, months of piecing together the puzzle that was Juliette Morrow, it was difficult to turn off that level of inquiry. He knew what she was, how she operated. It was natural to question why she chose the life she did.

But it was dangerous to begin caring about the answers.

"Before we go any further, we need to get some terms clear."

His brow raised at her cool tone. After taking another bite of eggs and washing it down with Scotch, he said, "And they are?"

"You threatened to send my grandmother to prison. That's ludicrous. She's an eighty-year-old woman with a heart condition. My cooperation depends upon her immediate release. She'll leave the country if you want. I can't concentrate if I'm worrying about her, as well."

"I'll alleviate that worry in any way I can, but she's going to remain in Paris. Somehow I think her presence nearby will ensure your cooperation, rather than provide a distraction. And as it happens, I believe we can build a strong case that your grandmother has been your accomplice all these years."

If he hadn't been watching her so carefully, he would have missed her reaction to his words. Her mouth trembled for an instant, just one, before she firmed it.

Sam took another sip of Scotch and pushed aside a niggling feeling that felt suspiciously like guilt. He'd done worse things during his years on the job than to play on a woman's love for her grandmother.

And God knew, Juliette had done worse things herself. So he wasn't going to regret the actions he'd taken to ensure her cooperation. Not any of them.

At any rate, she bounced back admirably. With an edge to her voice she demanded, "Then I demand that I be able to see her. Talk to her."

That he could grant her. "I'll take you to her later. What else?"

Juliette's gaze turned speculative. "If I'm successful with this job you have in mind, I want the necklace back."

"Most would think my destroying the file on you would be reward enough."

"Oh, you'll do that, too." Her tone was grim.

"Yes." He looked her squarely in the eye. "I will." She couldn't be certain that he'd do any such thing, and she'd be a fool to trust him. He knew she wasn't a fool. But he hoped during their time together she'd discover that he was a man of his word. He had every intention of doing exactly as he promised.

Sam looked down, half-surprised to find that he'd finished the eggs and both sides of bacon. He leaned forward and found a plate of potatoes and started in on them. Some might have a problem with the messy deals that were required in order to preserve national security. It had always seemed simple enough to him. Life was a series of tradeoffs. In return for the landing of Oppenheimer, a threat of international magnitude, Juliette Morrow would be free to adopt a new identity. To continue her life selecting targets and robbing them of their valuables until she was inevitably caught. Inevitably tried. Inevitably found guilty. The ends justified these particular means.

But it was telling that it wasn't the choices he made that bothered him at the moment. It was the thought of Juliette spending a couple of decades in prison.

"The necklace," she prompted.

"Yes, the necklace." Her words served to jolt him back to reality in a way nothing else could. It was the prize that was important to her. He needed to remember that, rather than wasting any regret over her eventual end. They all made their choices. She'd have to live with hers.

"As it happens, that necklace is insured by Oppenheimer's own insurance company." He spoke in between bites of potatoes. "It suits my purposes to have one of his holdings take a hit this large. And it doesn't much matter to me that he's lost another prized possession. So it's possible that I could be persuaded to part with it. We'll call it a bonus, if I'm satisfied with this job's outcome."

Juliette said nothing in reply. She'd seen the way his eyes had cooled, heard the censure in his words. An explanation was on the tip of her tongue, and stubbornly she swallowed it. She didn't owe this man anything, especially the divulging of long-kept secrets. He'd crashed into her carefully planned life and wreaked havoc on it. Disrupted her schedule and set her time line back by weeks, if not months.

Yes, he could believe what he wanted of her. Draw conclusions based upon the illusion she'd created. As long as she was free at the end to finish what she'd started ten years ago. "Well, then, that's all that's important, isn't it?" Nonchalantly she began stacking the dishes he'd emptied onto the tray.

"Apparently." He handed her the plate he held. "I need a shower. Or better yet, a hot bath."

She stilled in the act of accepting the dish. "I'm sure if you call the front desk, they can find you a room."

"No need. I'm staying with you." He gave her a thin smile. "I trust you exactly as much as you trust me. That's to say, not at all. You and I are going to be joined at the hip for the duration of this assignment. Best get used to it."

She stood frozen, his words swirling around her. Slowly, with a care that didn't escape her, he rose. "But...there's no need. I've already agreed to cooperate." A feeling of desperation rose that owed nothing to their deal. "You can't stay. I don't want you here."

She was talking to his broad back. He was walking in the direction of the bedrooms. "It's not what I want either. But it's the way it has to be."

Setting the plate down on the tray she hurried in his wake and nearly bumped into him as he ducked back out of the first bathroom he'd come to. "This isn't acceptable." She made her voice as implacable as his had been. "You'd better get used to the fact that you aren't going to have everything your way. You can't..."

He turned around so suddenly that this time she did run into him. Placing both hands on her shoulders, he lowered his face to hers. "I am going to have everything my way, Juliette." There was a hint of a drawl in the way he pronounced her name that sent an involuntary shiver down her spine. "I'm in charge. Do you understand that? You are going to do exactly what I say, when I say it. And in return you get your life back eventually. You're in no position to bargain, or to make demands. The sooner you learn that the better for both of us.''

Their gazes did battle, but if he thought she was going to agree with his outrageous statements, he was doomed to disappointment. He released her and turned, heading down the hallway. When he ducked into her bedroom, she was compelled to follow. ''No, not that one...''

''A whirlpool.'' His tone was practically reverent. By the time she entered the adjoining bathroom behind him he'd already started the jets.

''Absolutely not. You aren't using my bathroom. There have to be some boundaries, Tremaine. And this is...what are you doing?''

He already had his shirt half-unbuttoned. ''This is really your fault, you know.''

Try as she might, Juliette couldn't tear her eyes away from the wedge of broad chest he was baring. ''How do you figure that?''

''Your kick on the roof caught me in a bad spot.'' His voice was sardonic as he dropped the shirt on the floor. ''But I kinda figure you knew that at the time.''

Dammit, he wasn't going to make her feel guilty. She forced her gaze off his heavily muscled torso, wide shoulders, impressive biceps. She'd known the night they met on the dance floor that he was favoring one leg. It had been instinct that had driven her to strike at his vulnerability, and she wouldn't apologize for it now. As a matter of fact, given a chance, she'd kick him again.

Her gaze fell to his dark shirt on the floor, with the necklace spilling out of the inner pocket. The temptation to grab it and run, fast and far, was nearly dizzying. She was familiar with the layout of the hotel. It was possible she could outrun him. But it wouldn't change anything. Even if she could get away from Tremaine, get a new identity, start a new life, her grandmother would remain behind.

And there was no way she would abandon the only person in the world who loved her.

The sound of his zipper shattered her thoughts. Her gaze bounced back to him incredulously. He'd already kicked off his shoes and socks and his loosened dark pants were clinging precariously to his narrow hips. "This is a little more togetherness than I have in mind."

"Really? There's plenty of room for two in that tub." There was a devilish look in his eyes. He knew exactly how uncomfortable he was making her. That realization alone forced her to stay her ground, school her expression to polite boredom.

"I know exactly how much room there is in that tub." She manufactured a throaty laugh. "As a matter of fact, I can also tell you how long the hot water holds out. In case you're interested."

"I'm interested in anything you have to say, Juliette." The pants slid down long hard legs. He was left wearing only form-fitting black boxers, the sort that left little—very little—to the imagination. Something told her that after this scene her imagination was going to be very active indeed.

He grabbed the towel bar with one hand and stepped into the tub. Her gaze went to his injured leg and she nearly gasped aloud. She didn't know what she'd expected, but it wasn't the jagged angry-looking scar that traced down his thigh. It started just beneath his hip and was at least eight inches long. Still red, it looked to be fairly recent. And as close as it was to a major artery, it had to have been a life-threatening injury.

Throat dry, she could only stare as he stepped the rest of the way into the tub, hissing out a breath at the temperature, before easing himself down to a sitting position. Then he leaned his head back and closed his eyes, the picture of a healthy, blissful male animal.

"You know what would make this perfect?"

Somehow, she managed to swallow. Not trusting her voice, she merely shook her head.

"If you'd refill that glass of Scotch and bring it in here to me." He opened his eyes long enough to aim a coaxing look at her.

Without a word, she turned and went to fetch his glass, using the opportunity to draw a deep breath. She'd always prided herself on her ability to think on her feet. Instinct had driven her for so long, it was the primary sense she relied on. But right now she felt like she were standing on quicksand, with the earth constantly shifting and moving beneath her.

Her hand was not quite steady as she poured the Scotch. Crossing to the freezer, she withdrew some ice cubes and dropped them into the glass. Had it not been for her grandmother, she'd take her chances and make her escape right now. But Tremaine held the trump card, and he knew it. Her head was whirling, but try as she might, she couldn't think of one other way out of the surreal situation she found herself in.

She stood in the kitchen a moment longer, her hand clasping and releasing around the glass. When cornered, her instincts were to evade, bluff or parry.

She didn't capitulate to trouble, she punched her way out. There were options here; there had to be. And once she had more information, those options would become apparent to her.

She took a breath. Right now, however, much as she hated to admit it, her choices were depressingly limited. The realization, dismal as it was, was unavoidable. With reluctance weighing every muscle, she squared her shoulders, turned and retraced her steps, returning with the freshened drink to the half-naked man lounging in her whirlpool.

Chapter 4

"Juliette." Pauline rose from the table at the outdoor cafe and gave her granddaughter a hug. The gracefulness of her movements were in contrast to the fierceness with which she gripped the younger woman. "Are you all right?"

"Of course, Grandmama." Juliette returned her grandmother's hug and whispered, "I'll make this go away. Just give me time."

"Ms. Fontaine, I trust your accommodations have been comfortable." At Sam's smooth voice, the two women reluctantly broke apart and looked at him.

Pauline's brows arched. "Not as comfortable as my own home, no."

He inclined his head lazily, and held out a chair for Juliette. Once she'd sat, he waited for Pauline to reseat herself before sliding into his own chair. "You'll have to forgive my tactics. Juliette can be a bit...stubborn."

Pauline eyed him with an expression that Juliette knew all too well. "You mean because she didn't fall all over herself to cooperate with you? We're both well aware of the lengths some men will go to get what they want. Your actions are despicable, but hardly surprising."

If Sam was bothered by the censure in Pauline Fontaine's voice, it didn't show. His tone was respectful when he answered. "I think you are a practical woman, as well as a very beautiful one, Ms. Fontaine. One does what one must, wouldn't you say?"

Juliette looked sharply at him. Her grandmother frequently said that very thing, and she wondered if his words were coincidence or if they stemmed from the research he'd claimed to have done. At any rate, he had her grandmother pegged. Pauline was pragmatic to a fault. If he'd thought to be treated to hysterics and demands, he'd be sorely mistaken. The older woman was regarding him with a cool steady gaze.

"What I would say is that you're a man sorely lacking in breeding. Hardly surprising for an American."

"My own grandmother would wince to hear you say so. Honesty forces me to admit she did her best to teach me manners. Her lessons didn't always take." He lifted the plate of assorted cheeses and fruits from the table and began loading some on the plate in front of Juliette. When she made a protest, he sent her a narrowed look. "You didn't touch a thing room service brought, which means you haven't had a meal since yesterday. You'll eat. Or, if you like, I can feed you."

The glare she threw him would have withered most men. It had no noticeable effect on him. With ill grace, she picked up a piece of cheese, laid it on a cracker and lifted it to her mouth, biting it with restrained ferocity. Listening to his orders had quickly worn thin. That, if nothing else, should motivate her to think of a way out of this mess. And quickly.

She looked up then and caught her grandmother eyeing her and Sam speculatively. "Have you been treated well, Grandmama?"

Pauline raised a hand dismissively. "Don't spend your time worrying about me. I can take care of myself, I assure you. It would appear that you have enough to concern yourself about with…" She raised a brow in Sam's direction.

He filled in the pause smoothly. "Sam Tremaine, ma'am."

"Your name doesn't interest me as much as who you represent."

As Juliette opened her mouth to answer, he said, "Let's just agree that I'm Juliette's partner for the time being, and leave it at that." He leaned forward to pick up the bottle of wine the waiter had left for them and tipped some more into the older woman's glass.

Next he picked up the flute before Juliette and filled it as he continued to address Pauline. "Your granddaughter was worried about you. I promised her this meeting to assure her of your well-being. After this there will be no contact between the two of you until our association has come to an end."

Juliette raised the glass before her and noted wryly, "Given our separation I'm beginning to believe you've gotten the better end of the deal, Grand-mama. Mr. Tremaine has an annoying habit of issuing orders and expecting immediate obedience.'' She was surprised to see a tiny smile curve her grandmother's mouth.

''Oh dear, how trying for you, darling.''

''She doesn't appear too experienced at taking direction,'' Sam observed, sipping some water. ''But I think we'll be able to work out a mutually beneficial arrangement.'' With a deliberate shift of topic he inquired about the other woman's accommodations. Were they to her liking? Was there anything she needed? Was she being treated courteously?

Juliette flicked a glance at him as he made the inquiries. Were they really supposed to believe he cared one way or another about the answers? But there was a note of sincerity in his voice, and he gave every impression of being interested in her grandmother's replies. His head was inclined toward the older woman, and he was listening intently.

The umbrella over their table shielded them from the worst of the afternoon's brightness, but his position as he leaned forward placed him in a direct ray of sunlight, turning his hair a blinding shade of gold. It highlighted his hard profile, with its slash of cheekbones, hard lean jaw and straight blade of a nose.

Her gaze lingered for a moment longer. There was a slight bump on this side of his nose, below the bridge, hinting at an old break. Abruptly she remembered the jagged, barely healed wound on his leg, and knew both injuries were only two on a long list. There had been an assortment of faded scars patterning his muscled body, and she'd been treated to a fine view of them before she'd left him to soak. Separately, each of the injuries would tell a fascinating story. Together they hinted at a life of violence she didn't want to consider. There was too much she didn't know about Sam Tremaine. But it was rapidly becoming clear that he was more—much more—than he claimed to be.

She did know he worked fast. They hadn't been in her apartment an hour that morning before his luggage had arrived, implying a sense of permanence that even now stung. She guessed he was smart, mercenary and more than a little fierce when provoked. And she knew that despite his injury, he was in prime physical condition.

Her throat suddenly dry, Juliette tipped her glass to her lips, and forced her attention back to the couple at the table. Sam was writing something on a card and handing it to her grandmother. "If you need anything at all you can contact me at this number, day or night. One of my associates will dial it for you."

Pauline slowly took the card. "So I'm to enjoy my gilded cage for the duration, hmm?"

"As much as possible, ma'am."

The older woman tucked the card in the small bag she carried. "Perhaps a few of your grandmother's lessons were not in vain, after all."

Sam's hard mouth curved. "Mostly the ones she accentuated with willow switches, ma'am, but she'd be proud to hear you say so."

"Willow switches?" Juliette sipped at her wine, her interest piqued despite herself. "I think she should have tried something longer and stouter if she wanted to make more of an impression."

"Bloodthirsty little thing, aren't you?" His gaze

met hers over the top of his glass, a glimmer of amusement evident.

"Not at all. I've just noted a certain single-mind-edness that may be the result of lack of discipline as a child."

He touched his glass to hers, surprising her. "Something we have in common, then."

Deliberately, she placed her wineglass back on the table. She wouldn't give him the satisfaction of drinking to that remark. He couldn't possibly realize the experiences that had shaped her, and she was beginning to resent his insinuations. From the little he'd said, he'd been on Oppenheimer's trail for a long time, as well. They had that in common, and regardless of his motivation, she doubted her goals were any less noble than his.

A capricious breeze sent a strand of hair dancing, and her hand rose to smooth it back from her face. Her fingers met Sam's as he reached out at that moment to do the same. She froze, her gaze jerking to his. The act was curiously intimate, and from the expression on his face, he was as surprised by the impulse as she was.

He dropped his hand and turned back to her grand-mother, and after a moment she did the same. It would be difficult to miss the gleam of interest in Pauline's eyes, and Juliette didn't regret that the sit-uation made it impossible for her to have a private moment or two with her grandmother. She didn't feel up to parrying the older woman's questions.

With a discreet movement, she shifted her chair so Sam's leg wasn't brushing against hers. Whether these too casual touches were deliberate or not, she wouldn't allow them to haze her logic. That was one area she could control, and she would. Sam Tremaine could charm the thorns off roses. Already there was an almost imperceptible softening in her grand-mother, and Lord knew, the woman was as intuitive as they came.

But he wouldn't charm Juliette. She reached for her glass and drank, silently toasting the vow. Tremaine had shown himself to be ruthless about getting what he wanted. She could identify with that quality, even respect it on some level. She possessed a certain measure of ruthlessness herself. But the man hadn't been born who could make her lose focus, to distract her from her objective.

And no man in the world could make her forget.

With barely concealed impatience she waited as small talk was made, contributing very little to it. The carafe of wine was slowly emptied, the tray of afternoon cheese and crackers eaten and her attention drifted to the two men at a table a discreet distance from theirs. Although out of earshot, their chairs were arranged to keep Tremaine's table in sight, and she knew intuitively that the men belonged to him; the associates he'd spoken of. No doubt they served as her grandmother's captors, as well. Studying them, Juliette saw nothing remarkable in their appearance. Nondescript features, neither tall nor short, they wouldn't stand out in a crowd. She knew exactly how important that quality was. Tremaine obviously did, too.

When her grandmother finally rose to go, Juliette barely managed to restrain a sigh of relief. That sigh became a strangled gasp when the older woman hugged her again and murmured, ''He's not indifferent to you, darling. A wise woman would use that. Sex can be an effective tool.''

''Grandmother...''

The rest of her words slid down her throat when fingers closed over her elbow and a low voice said, ''Ready?''

Juliette glanced up to find Sam's face much too close to hers. Had he overheard her grandmother's whispered suggestion? Heat suffused her. She yanked her arm from his grasp and preceded him through the cafe. Embarrassment was a wasted, useless emotion, one she rarely indulged in. She refused to do so now. A woman in her position would be stupid not to consider using any weapon at her disposal to get the upper hand. Juliette didn't lack intelligence.

But neither was she jaded enough to sleep with someone in an effort to exert control over them. She wondered if Tremaine could say the same.

Once in the car she didn't speak for several minutes. ''This isn't the way back to my apartment.''

''No.'' The late afternoon sun slanting into the vehicle dusted his whole body with a bronze glow, giving his poet's face an almost saintly look. Her mouth twisted. That only went to show how far apart nature and reality were.

''I'm taking you to meet another associate of mine.''

Although his words were uttered matter-of-factly enough, she felt anticipation rise. ''Am I finally going to be given all the details of this job? It's about time.''

''Juliette.'' He managed to sound wounded. ''One would think you didn't appreciate my efforts on your behalf this afternoon. Didn't seeing your grand-mother put some of your concerns to rest?''

''I'd almost believe that was your intent if I didn't realize that the meeting suited your own purpose.''

Taking wire-framed sunglasses off the dash, he flipped them open and put them on. ''And what purpose might that be?''

''To provide a potent reminder of just what I stand to lose by not cooperating with you.''

Sam shook his head sadly. ''You have a cynical outlook. Sad in one so young.'' He handled the car expertly in the Parisian traffic, navigating the narrow streets like a pro. ''I'd ask what shaped it, but you don't trust me enough to tell me. Not yet.''

The inflection he gave the last word was imbued with certainty, as though it were just a matter of time before she'd divulge all sorts of personal details for his dissection. If he truly believed that, he wasn't as intelligent as she'd given him credit for.

They pulled to a stop before a tall narrow building. Weather had washed the brick to a pale rose, so it stood out among the neighboring buildings like a faded bloom. The crowded surroundings didn't disguise the quiet elegance of the neighborhood. It shimmered wealth.

She looked around with interest as Sam unlocked the door and ushered her inside. The promise of elegance outside was reflected in the furnishings and the decorations. A Matisse adorned the wall next to her, and with only a quick look she assessed both its authenticity and value. The mental summary was second nature, as unconscious as breathing. When they passed by a glassed collection of Fabergé eggs, she gave an inner nod of approval. Wealth was wasted on those without taste.

"Is this your home?"

Sam cocked a brow at her. "Do I look like old money?"

Juliette didn't even take a moment to consider her answer. "Yes." She couldn't say exactly what there was about him that hinted at it. He obviously was accustomed to the best, but those habits could be acquired later in life. It was more a sense of belonging. Even dressed casually as he was right now, in khakis and a short-sleeved green polo shirt that hugged his biceps, he appeared at home in the place. If he didn't live here, he lived somewhere much like it. It really wasn't difficult to identify the people born to this kind of life. Just as it was glaringly obvious which of them were not.

Don't touch anything! This is as close to class as white trash like you will ever come.

The voice slid beneath the door she'd slammed on that particular memory, sly and sneering. The words still had vicious little barbs, and stung as deeply.

"Juliette?"

With a jerk she looked at Sam, shoving the memory back in a corner of her mind. "What?"

"I said it belongs to a friend. I just have the use of it for a while."

Completely recovered now, she moved easily by him. "Some friend." Once out of the spacious hallway she found herself in a huge living room. Aside from the small kitchen tucked into one corner of the home, the space took up the rest of the floor. This room, too, was filled with priceless antiques and works of art. But it was the man standing near the fireplace who drew her attention.

"Juliette, meet Miles Caladesh, an associate of mine."

She slanted Sam a glance. "You do seem to have a number of them, don't you?" Something besides his expressionless tone alerted her. He hadn't bothered to introduce her to the men guarding her grandmother, and they obviously weren't enjoying the opulent generosity of Sam's friend. Something about this man was different. Instincts, always just below the surface, began to hum. Now, perhaps, she'd get the details about the job Tremaine thought was so important.

The stranger was staring at her, long enough to be considered rude. Rather than let it bother her, Juliette moved into the room and seated herself on a long curved couch that was every bit as comfortable as it looked.

Clearing his throat, the other man said, "You're not what I expected."

She crossed her legs. "I won't ask what you did expect, since the answer is sure to be offensive."

Sam seated himself in a chair near the couch and watched Caladesh cynically. It wasn't difficult to imagine the cause of the man's unusual speechlessness. Juliette made an impression, and it was all too evident that she'd made one on Miles. There was a burn low in his gut that he refused to identify as jealousy. Emotion had no place in his life, at least not while he was working. And allowing emotion to creep into his dealings with Juliette would be more than dangerous, it'd be downright disastrous.

He forced his mind off that train of thought and

got ready to do damage control if necessary. Caladesh, damn him, seemed intent on micromanaging every detail of this operation. Since Headquarters had already approved their use of Juliette for this job, there was very little to be gained from this meeting.

Obviously recovered, Miles raked her up and down with a glance. "So you're the notorious thief wanted on three continents by some of the most powerful law enforcement agencies in the world. Are they all really that inept or are you that good?"

"I'm that good," she responded without hesitation, and Sam allowed himself a small smile. Beneath the stunning packaging was a healthy ego. Having her identity discovered had probably sliced at it more than a bit. But it hadn't altered her confidence at its most basic level. Even while he despised the choices she made he could appreciate the sheer guts, daring and intelligence necessary for her to be so successful at her chosen work.

Miles folded his arms across his chest. "Let's hope you're half as skilled as you think you are, and it was just Tremaine's good fortune that led him to uncover your identity so easily."

Her gaze narrowed and Sam tensed, wondering if he'd have to intervene. He'd seen signs of Juliette's temper, although she'd always managed to leash it. But if she decided to take on Miles, he'd place his bets on her.

Her voice was even enough when she answered. "Make up your mind, Mr. Caladesh. Is it my skills you're disparaging or Tremaine's?"

"Just determining whether you're up to this job we have in mind." Miles reached in his suit jacket and took out a slender platinum case. Extracting a slim French cigarette, he put it between his lips and lit it before adding, ''We have a lot riding on this. How much has Tremaine told you?''

Juliette settled a bit deeper into the couch cushions and glanced at Sam. ''I know Hans Oppenheimer has something you think I can get for you.''

''Correction, Ms. Morrow, something you *will* get for us.'' Miles leaned forward to flick ash into a decorative dish on a nearby table. ''If you refuse or fail you'll find your pretty behind in prison for a very, very long time.''

The only sign of Juliette's reaction was the casual swing of her foot, but Sam wasn't fooled. Beneath the layer of calm she'd be seething. What Miles saw as a show of power would only antagonize their best hope for nailing Oppenheimer. Not for the first time in recent weeks, he cursed bureaucracy politics. Because of his connections, Caladesh had bounced from agency to agency, adding impressively to his resume while acquiring very little actual knowledge. It was damn certain he'd never had any experience with agents or contacts.

He thought it wise to take over the conversation. ''The take this time won't be as exciting as your usual targets, I'm afraid. We're just after information. You get in, find the file we need and get out again. Oppenheimer can't know that anyone was ever there.''

''And the information in this file…'' She looked at both men in turn. ''Why is it so important to you?''

''You'd do well not to think about questions like that, Ms. Morrow.'' Caladesh walked to a chair and sat down, meticulously smoothing the creases from his trousers. "At any rate, you won't be going in alone. We just need your expertise in gaining access. Sam will find the pertinent files once you gain entry."

Nerves jittered in her stomach. *Sam?* Sam would be going in with her? He'd neglected to mention that detail, but then, it appeared that there was a great deal neither man was willing to tell her.

"Mr. Tremaine has a certain level of expertise in that area himself," she said coolly, remembering his surprising presence in the gallery. "Why do you need me?"

"I'm afraid his experience in the area doesn't rise to the level this case will entail." Caladesh drew on his cigarette again.

"Which of Oppenheimer's offices are you targeting?" He had more than a dozen, she knew, in as many different countries. And that wasn't taking into account the headquarters for the various corporations he owned.

"None of them. The evidence we seek is kept on his Austrian estate."

Caladesh's words seemed to sound through a vacuum. The playing field leveled with a dizzying abruptness. "State of the art security there, but I'm sure you know that." She studied each man's face in turn. "The attack dogs don't pose much of a problem, and the CCTV surveillance can be dealt with. The alarm system is a Gravoc Protective Circuit system, which is difficult, but not impossible. It's the reinforced Tru-Secure vault that's the real problem. Cutting edge, it's blast proof and drill proof."

She paused a moment to enjoy the men's expressions, but it was Sam she watched most carefully. He looked unsurprised, even satisfied.

"You've researched the security on his estate." The words weren't phrased as a question, but she nodded anyway.

"I have schematics of all the systems, and blueprints of the house." She studied her nails nonchalantly. "Unless you can say the same, I imagine my sharing them would save you a great deal of time, not to mention considerable expense." She aimed a look at Sam. "But it's going to cost you."

"Of course it is." It was difficult to tell from his tone whether he was amused or resigned. But there was no missing the emotion in Caladesh's words.

"It's not going to cost us a thing." They both looked at the other man. "You'll hand them over, and count it a payment toward retaining your freedom."

"Wrong. My help in obtaining that evidence in Oppenheimer's vault is the price for that file you have on me. If you want the information I have, that's going to be a different transaction."

"And I bet I can imagine what price you have in mind."

There was no missing the cynicism in Sam's remark, but Juliette held his gaze steadily. "You'll have access to everything I have on the Oppenheimer estate, and in return…you'll let my grandmother leave the country."

He blinked. That was his only reaction, but she knew intuitively that she'd managed to surprise him. Time suspended and she barely breathed as she awaited his answer.

"You know I can't do that."

Crushing disappointment welled, threatened to swamp her. It was a moment before she could force words around the boulder-size knot in her throat. "Your choice. I'm sure you have other contacts who can get you the same information." She forced her limbs to relax, as if it didn't matter. "Unless, of course, time is an element."

The two men exchanged a look before Sam said, "There's no denying the value of your research. Given your relationship with Oppenheimer, I was counting on you to have something we could use."

Her gaze jerked to his. "My relationship?"

"We know you've targeted him, and his holdings. It would go to figure that you'd have information about his security that we'd be interested in."

Nerves were still bumping in her veins. "Information isn't free."

"There'll be no deals." Caladesh ground his cigarette out in the dish. "My God, we've got the upper hand. You don't seem to understand your position here, Morrow."

She didn't respond; there was no need. Juliette didn't know what part the other man played in this, but she was counting on Tremaine to be more reasonable. So it was to him she addressed her next words. "He's wrong. I understand my position perfectly, and I think you do, too. So start figuring what my research is worth to you. Because it doesn't come without a price."

Chapter 5

"It's out of the question."

Juliette whirled on Sam as he was closing the door to her penthouse behind him. "You sound like a broken record. Why are you so opposed to my grandmother's release? She has nothing to do with this job you want me for."

"She has everything to do with it," he disputed. Crossing to the thermostat, he adjusted the air-conditioning. "If I allow her to leave the country, you'd follow her at the earliest opportunity."

"I gave you my word I'd see this job through." She uttered the lie without batting an eyelash. Family superseded promises made in desperation.

So it shouldn't have offended her so much when Sam replied, "You'll forgive me if I don't find your word particularly compelling. Once this job is over you and your grandmother will be free to go wherever you wish, but not before then."

Her fist clenched in an unconscious gesture of frustration. It would have given her a great deal of satisfaction to take a swing at him. The glint in his eye told her he knew it, too. "I could, however, be persuaded to make a trade for the information you've put together."

Temper shifted aside a fraction. She eyed him speculatively. "The only other thing you have that I'm interested in is the necklace."

He inclined his head. "Exactly. You can have it back now if your research is as detailed as you claim."

Dropping her purse on the Chippendale table, she considered his offer. Her desire to get the necklace didn't come close to matching her wish to get her grandmother far, far away from all this. Failure, or even worse, capture, was a possibility in any job. It was one thing to put herself at risk, but if this should end badly how could she be assured of her grandmother's freedom? What guarantee did she have that Pauline would be released as promised?

"I'll agree to trade the research on Oppenheimer's security for the necklace." She sat down in an armchair, made a production of crossing her ankles. "If you'll agree to release my grandmother as soon as we're on the Oppenheimer estate."

He immediately looked wary. "What's the difference if she's released when we go in or once we get out?"

She smiled coolly. "Let's call it a trust issue. Her release is not going to be contingent upon the success of this job."

"If you're worried about what Miles said earlier…"

"Of the two of you, I trust him even less, so yes, he worries me. I don't want him changing the rules midgame."

He lowered himself into a chair. If she hadn't been watching him so closely, she wouldn't have noticed the care he took in the action. His leg was probably hurting him again. She refused to allow herself to care. "All right."

She stared at him, suspicious at the easy capitulation. "All right?"

"We'll both get what we want. I don't make the phone call until we're safely inside, though."

"It would work better to make it while we were still outside the wall," she pointed out, satisfaction mingling with relief. "We don't need any extra noise once we're in."

He eyed her lazily. "You aren't the only one experiencing a serious lack of trust. How do I know you'll follow through once she's released?"

There was no reason to feel a sting at his remark. She lifted her chin. "Fine. We'll compromise. When we're on the grounds you'll make the call."

"Once you've deactivated the alarm system," he countered.

She settled back in her chair, crossed her leg and started swinging her foot. "I get to talk to her."

He inclined his head. "All right." He waited an instant, allowing her time to decide. But there was really no decision to be made. It was the best deal she was going to get from him, and she knew it. But that didn't preclude pushing for more later. She smiled brilliantly. "Fine."

He stared at for a moment, then shook his head a little. "That's dangerous."

"What?"

"That smile. It's designed to blind the eye and dazzle the senses, isn't it? You're very beautiful."

"The way you say it, it isn't a compliment."

His mouth curved but his gaze was cynical. "I'm sure you're used to compliments. I'm just as certain that you find them empty."

The accuracy of his remark was a shock, and arrowed much too close to the truth. She shook her hair back, aimed a look at him from beneath her lashes. "You don't know women very well if you believe that."

"We're not talking about other women, though, are we? We're talking about you." He hitched one ankle up on the opposite knee. "Oh, I don't doubt that you use your beauty when it's to your advantage, but it's a tool to you. One to be wielded with every bit as much skill as that glass cutter you used in the gallery."

It was sheer strength of will that kept her seated, her voice amused. "And you're so different? With those Greek god looks of yours and that air of mystery? I'm sure you find yourself tripping over women."

Real humor chased into his eyes. "I usually try to be a bit more subtle than that. But if you want to see if I'm susceptible to sweet nothings, feel free. I'll attempt to be strong."

She wanted, badly, to smile. A genuine one this time, and because the humor behind it was real, she was determined to restrain it. He needed no encouragement. "What are you hiding behind that polished charm and those golden boy looks, Tremaine?" She was satisfied to see his amusement fade as his expression went guarded. "Perhaps we're not so different. You don't want anyone poking around beneath the surface, either. Otherwise you wouldn't work so hard to make people believe that the surface is all there is. And you are, after all, little more than a thief yourself."

She waited for a reaction, but when none was forthcoming, she added, "Or perhaps would-be thief is a more appropriate term. You have the desire, but lack the skills to do the job yourself."

"We're different in one very fundamental way." Sam ignored the lazy arching of her eyebrows, inviting him to go on. There was very little more to add. She was more intuitive than he would have given her credit for, but then he shouldn't be surprised. He'd never doubted her intelligence, only her ethics. And she was right, there *were* similarities between them. He'd noted them himself as he'd compiled the data on her, one piece at a time. They both wore masks, concealing their true purposes from the outside world. For him, it was a way of life, a necessity in the performance of his job. He supposed she would say the same. But he tended to think that matters of national security superseded personal greed as a motivator, so in that way they couldn't be more different.

"What exactly is in this file you're so interested in, anyway? Business secrets, corporate espionage?" She sounded curious. "Are you a rival of Oppenheimer's?"

"You could say that." Enemy would be a far more descriptive adjective, thanks to Sterling's duplicity. They had no way of knowing if he'd revealed Sam's identity, or those of the other agents who'd answered to him. No way to be certain how badly the investigation had been compromised. But they had to assume Oppenheimer knew everything Sterling had known. Which had necessitated the top secrecy of this mission. And ratcheted up the risk, accordingly.

She rose. "Since you don't seem disposed to explaining that last remark, I'll go get those security specs."

"You keep them here?"

"It's safer here than it would be most places." When he started to rise, she stopped him. "You get the necklace. I'm going to want it before I hand this information over to you."

He allowed her to exit without comment, and because he'd never denied being male, took the time to appreciate the view. There were, he decided, few women who looked so damn good walking away. And not a little of her impact came from the fact that she wasn't trying to maximize it. It was as if, with their earlier conversation, they had come to some sort of understanding. Wariness was still going to color their relationship. Neither of them were naive. But a layer of pretense had been dropped, as they'd discussed the job. Juliette was nothing if not a businesswoman. He found he could respect that, if very little else about her.

Taking advantage of her absence, he went to her purse, and after a quick glance to assure himself he was still alone, removed the miniscule high-powered listening device he'd placed in it at the consulate party before he'd ever approached her. With a quirk of his lips, he thought about how furious she'd be if she found out how he'd managed to follow her to Denmark. The discovery might well elicit another tantrum, with the items she heaved aimed at him this time.

With an amused shake of his head, he pocketed the bug and withdrew an equally small tracking device. Attaching it to the underside of the zipper, he checked it for secureness, before setting her purse back in place. It had been a kick in the ego for her to accept that he'd managed to follow her, but she'd recover. There were other, far more important things at stake.

He went to the master bedroom, *her* bedroom, to pull his bags from the closet. From the false bottom of one, he withdrew the necklace and held it up a moment to admire it. There was no denying its beauty, its obvious value, but aside from that it left him cold. It meant something to Juliette, however. Probably because of those two qualities, and it'd be best to keep that in mind. She might have surprised him by putting her grandmother's safety above the retrieval of the necklace, but it hadn't taken long for her to make the demand for it, as well. He'd do well to remember that.

A slight noise alerted him. He looked up, listening sharply as his hand went to his ankle holster. It was rarely necessary for him to carry a weapon, but Sterling's betrayal had changed a lot of things. Drawing the gun, he rose, senses still attuned. But the noise wasn't coming from outside this room. It was closer than that.

Comprehension punched in. He leaned down, slipped the gun back in its holster, and walked farther into the closet. It was what his sister would refer to as a walk-in, which in Sam's opinion just meant a small room to keep far more clothes than any one person should ever need. He'd looked through the racks and sets of shelves and then paused when the slight noises sounded louder.

He smiled broadly. There was a bit more to the space than dress after dress. He reached out, rubbed the fabric of one little red number between his fingers and stifled a mental image of what Juliette would look like in the skimpy garment. Crouching down, he examined the shelves that held more shoes than any woman could wear in this lifetime. There was a whirring sound, and he watched the entire section of shelves move inward on unseen hinges. Juliette started to step through the opening, arms full, and then froze when she saw him there.

He reached out, hooked a high heeled red sandal that consisted of little more than straps, and let it dangle from one crooked finger. "I don't suppose you have this in a twelve."

Faster than he dreamed possible, she was through the opening, giving him a good shove with one foot that had him teetering in his crouched position. "Let's get something straight, Tremaine. You're going to respect some boundaries here, or we're going to part ways right now."

He refrained from pointing out that they were well beyond that point and looked past her to the space she'd just exited. "A hidden room. No wonder you weren't worried about keeping that stuff here." He leaned past her to peer more closely. "Reinforced steel inlay?" He let out a low whistle. The door slid shut after that first glimpse. "Very nice. And expensive. Of course, I don't have to ask if your pastime has been profitable."

She walked past him, her spine stiff. He spent a

moment longer examining the woodwork for a release mechanism, then looked up, caught her glaring at him.

"Sorry." His sheepish shrug wiped none of the fury from her face. Deciding discretion was definitely the better part of valor in this case, he rose, approached her. "Need any help with that?" She turned and stalked out of the closet leaving him to trail in her wake. "So what's it run on? Flip pin? Delayed circuit?"

"Combination keypad, and don't even think about it," she warned as he looked over his shoulder.

He looked back at her and strove for an innocent expression. "Me? I was just interested in the shoes."

"Somehow I doubt it." He strolled after her as she strode back into the living room. The keypad must be well hidden, or else he would have seen it before she'd stepped out. His fingers itched. He had a few skills in covert access himself, but it wasn't the challenge her secret room presented that tempted him, it was the contents. He supposed it was a safe enough place to keep anything she took while she was waiting to resell it, or whatever she did with her take.

What else would Juliette Morrow prize enough to keep hidden away from the rest of the world? Other people's valuables? Or something more personal? The fact that the questions were so intriguing should worry him. He didn't spend time wondering about his contacts' personal lives, but then Juliette wasn't his usual contact. That in itself should scare the hell out of him.

She went to the dining table and set down the box she was carrying. Withdrawing a narrow tube, she twisted off the top and withdrew a set of rolled-up papers. He helped her spread them flat and saw that they were blueprints. Interest sharpening, he leaned closer to study them more intently. "Layouts of Oppenheimer's home?"

She nodded with a trace of smugness. "They didn't come cheap, I can tell you that. If you don't mind," she said, reaching over and snatching the necklace from his hand. "I'll take that."

"Looks like a fair enough exchange," he murmured. Almost absently he noted that her accent had all but disappeared. He may not have nailed exactly where she was from, but he'd bet money he'd been close. He knew an American speech pattern when he heard one. Tracing his index finger along the red lines that had been drawn in marker, he saw that she'd made notations on the sheets, in a clean bold script that somehow suited her. *Power cables. Server. Annunciator.* According to the blueprints the entire home was well over twenty-five thousand square feet. Not a bad place for a guy who'd never done an honest hour's work in his life.

Juliette left the room, he assumed to put the necklace away for safekeeping. He reached into the box and withdrew a bulging manilla envelope. Inside were schematics for the security system. Another envelope held notes of the CCTV system, the number of computers and pictures of the employees and their hours. With a slight frown on his face, he looked in the direction of the bedroom. She hadn't been overstating the extent of the information she had on the estate. He'd guessed she'd have some—it only went to figure that a thief who'd been targeting Oppenheimer for as long as she had would eventually hit his home. But the wealth of information she had here opened up a whole new set of questions.

She reentered the room, stopping short when she saw him staring at her. "What?"

"Have you been inside Oppenheimer's estate before?"

Resuming her approach, she shook her head. "No. But it pays to be prepared, doesn't it?"

Her offhand tone didn't fool him. "So you've been preparing to strike his main home. What's stopped you?"

Lifting a shoulder, she joined him at the table. "The time wasn't right."

"What have you been waiting for?"

Her gaze shifted. "This information isn't free, you know. It takes a great deal of money in the right places to come up with these details."

Her evasion was obvious, but he let it go for the movement. "How much do these vaults cost?"

"Two hundred thousand retail, maybe half that black market."

Miles would have to run the expense by Headquarters, but given what hung in the balance, he didn't think it would be a problem. "I could get one for you by tomorrow, but you'll only have a matter of hours to work on it. I assume you'd have to figure out how to spring the combination."

"Hours?" She gave an incredulous laugh. "It isn't a piggy bank, Tremaine. Regardless of what you think of my career, it does require a bit of skill."

He thought it best not to comment on her skills, and how she'd acquired them. "Our schedule is going to be dictated by Oppenheimer's. Right now he's in Germany, but I believe once his business there is taken care of, he plans to go to his estate.''

He'd managed to capture her attention. ''How do you know that?''

Smiling grimly, he said, ''You're not the only one who pays for intelligence. My point is, we have a narrow window of opportunity in which to act. It has to be before he gets there and removes the file.''

''If that's true, you're right. We have to act fast. The problem is, his vault doesn't use a combination, it functions on an electronic keypad.''

''You mean like the door to your secret room.''

Scowling at him she suggested, ''Why don't you just forget about that?'' She propped her hip against the table, pulling her dress tighter. He'd have to be a saint not to notice the way it outlined her hips and the long line of her slender thighs. He stole a look, willing to live with the fact that he was a long way from being canonized.

''Keypads narrow the possibility of unauthorized entry. And since you want a soft access, we'll eliminate the use of C-4.''

''I thought you said it was blast proof.''

She waved off his words. ''What I'm getting at is that the type of access dictates our plan of action. There's only one way to open a keypad entry on that vault, and it's going to mean we need to have him there on the estate.''

''Not a chance. He travels with an entourage, so that's an increased number of people on the grounds, which increases our risk.'' If he had a mind to, he could tell her exactly how many people accompanied Oppenheimer at any given moment. He wondered if she didn't have the same sort of information herself.

She rose from her perch against the table and smoothed out the wrinkles in her dress. Made of a sheer flowery material, it fully covered her like a gauzy veil that made a man wish for a good stiff wind. He gave a moment's consideration to opening the window.

"The only way to accomplish a soft access to that vault is to apply invisible ultraviolet ink to something he has to touch before he opens it." Juliette rummaged through the box until she came to another envelope. Opening it, she withdrew some more schematics.

Leaning in, Sam saw computer drawings of a room. Looking up to meet her gaze, he said, "His office?"

She nodded. "As you can see here—" she stabbed a finger at the section she wanted to draw his attention to "—he has the vault enclosed behind a regular door which employs only a standard lock. I suppose he figures there's no real reason to expend much expense there when the vault itself is so secure. If I apply the UV ink to the doorknob, some residual ink will remain on his fingertips once he opens the door and punches in the code on the keypad." Her voice was growing more animated as she talked, her eyes brighter. "From there it's simply a matter of shining an ultraviolet lamp on the buttons to see which he pushed. I'll run a computer program on numerical sequences for three, four and five digit combinations. With that to consult, it shouldn't take me more than three or four tries to open it."

He stepped away, shoved his hands in his pockets. "I still don't like the amount of risk we're taking here." For the first time he considered how much

danger he was placing Juliette in. Frowning, he
moved away. Somehow he thought it'd be easier to
think if he put some distance between them. He was
using her to do a job in which she had expertise. It
was no different, he argued with himself, than if he'd
recruited a foreign secretary to pass on information
about her boss. And her background made her risk
more minimal; she was used to this kind of danger.
From all appearances, she thrived on it.

So why was there a burn deep in his gut that he
was the one placing her in jeopardy this time? He
shrugged off the answer that came readily to mind
as she spoke again. "If it's that important to you,
there's another way. It would mean going in twice,
the second time after he's left again, but…"

"No." With that word he accepted the risk. And
the responsibility. "We can't spare the time, and going in twice doubles our exposure." Rubbing his
temples, he considered the possibilities.

"You said you can find out when he plans to be
there." Juliette approached him as she spoke. "We'll
be prepared to act as soon as he does."

"I'd expect him to go to the vault shortly after he
arrives. He's a paranoid bastard…he's going to want
to take inventory." He sent a wry glance her way.
"Especially after the loss of that necklace."

A tiny smile settled on her lips, as if the memory
gave her a great deal of satisfaction. A bolt of lust
tightened through him. He'd been raised with a code
of honor that dictated every action he'd ever taken.
Honor. Duty. Devotion. Others might scoff at such
old-fashioned qualities, but for his family they were
a way of life. It would be more comfortable to believe that he could never be attracted to someone like

Juliette Morrow. Someone who was willing to circumvent laws and morals for her own personal gain. The opposite seemed true. Perhaps it was inevitable, with the amount of time he'd spent trailing her. An unwilling fascination had developed ever since he'd discovered the identity of *le petit voleur*.

It was a measure of that fascination, nothing more, that fueled this reluctant desire. And because he needed that to be true, he'd believe it.

Shoving emotion aside, he said, "You realize that means we'll have to be hidden inside for hours, maybe even overnight."

She lifted a shoulder. "You're not afraid of the dark, are you? Or of small enclosed places?"

Her daring tone pulled a smile from him. "I've never had either aversion, no."

"Because if you are," she leaned over, placed her palms on his chest, "I can always go in alone."

He reached up to capture her hands in his. "No need. What about you? Any problem with spending that long hiding in a small dark area…with me?"

Awareness flickered in her eyes, but her tone was still light when she answered. "I'm a professional. I can do whatever the job calls for."

"Good. That makes two of us."

Their words hung in the air between them, took on a second meaning. Currents of tension thrummed between them. Juliette tugged at her hands but he didn't let go of them. His eyes gleamed with an unmistakable lust. Her stomach abruptly hollowed when she identified his expression.

Hunger. Raw and powerful, it stilled her heart for an instant before lashing it to a fervent pace. She recognized the desire on his face. She was less familiar with the answering longing it evoked. Passion surged, threatened to claw free. The world felt as though it was spinning rapidly out of orbit, and the only thing that would right it was his kiss.

Going on tiptoe, she pressed her mouth against his, letting the dark, sensual flavor of him play havoc with her pulse. His hands released hers to slide around her waist. When he urged her closer, she went willingly, unthinkingly, until they were sealed against each other in a scalding band of heat. There were a few moments, as they lazily tasted each other, when she felt in control. She'd step back in a minute. Or in two. As soon as she'd had her fill of that un-mistakable sexual confidence that shimmered off him in waves.

His tongue pushed deep into her mouth in a long velvet glide and she welcomed the intimacy. He was a man who knew how to kiss a woman, she thought dizzily, deep and hot and wet, staking a claim. Soft one instant and rough the next, as if in the next second he intended to strip her bare and mount her for a long wild ride.

It was that thought that had her reining in her hormones. There was no trust here, on either side. He'd strong-armed her into helping him, and neither of them was willing to give an ounce of personal information to the other. When this was over they'd walk away, have no reason to see each other ever again. It would be stupid to reach out for more. Stupid to start to care, even a little.

Restraint had never been more difficult to summon. She dragged her lips from his, stiffened and tried to move away. And it was then that she found just how she'd been fooling herself when she'd thought, even for a moment, that she was in control.

His mouth went to her neck, and he scored the cord there with his teeth. A shudder worked through her as the muscles in her legs took on the consistency of warm wax. The filmy fabric of her dress was pushed aside to allow his hand to slide up her leg and cup her bottom. He squeezed the flesh beneath his palm rhythmically, as he strewed a string of kisses along her throat in quick stinging succession. She knew that the real danger of this job didn't lie in the break-in. It revolved around this man, and her fierce reaction to him.

His mouth settled on hers again for a raw, carnal kiss, implicit in its demand. She could feel her will ebb, as temptation beckoned. Whatever the outcome between them, this at least would be worth it. She had no doubts about that. What happened between them would be as wild as it would be unforgettable.

Later she would be ashamed that it was only that thought that had her tearing herself away from him. When this was over she'd turn and walk away, taking her life back with her. She'd start over, and continue on the path set long ago. The path she'd set for herself.

Breath heaving, she stared at him with huge eyes. *Unforgettable.* She didn't need the memories that would haunt long after the two of them had parted. Didn't want to be able to summon the taste of him, to remember the way she'd felt in his arms. Memories were nasty little thieves that snuck into the mind and distracted it from its focus.

And all too often those memories left a trail of scalding pain in their wake.

The skin was pulled tightly over his cheekbones, and his expression was primitive. A flush of arousal stained his cheekbones and his eyes glittered as brightly as the emeralds she'd once lifted from a showing in London.

"Lose your nerve?"

The rasp in his tone had her clasping her arms around herself, as if for support. Praying her legs would hold her, she backed away, unable to summon an answer.

"Your grandmother would be disappointed. She's right, sex can be an effective tool. Anytime you want to see if it works on me, feel free."

He turned away, headed back to the table. But Juliette didn't follow him. She couldn't. There was a trembling in her limbs that wouldn't allow her to move. He'd heard her grandmother earlier that day. The realization hammered in her head, followed by another, more frightening thought. Although he'd had no difficulty remembering Pauline's words, she hadn't thought of them for an instant while she'd been in his arms. Not once.

And that fact absolutely terrified her.

Chapter 6

"How soon do you need this?" Jacques didn't look up from the list he was scribbling.

"Today, if possible. I'm not sure how quickly I'll have to move."

He looked up then, stared hard at Juliette. "You're not sure?"

His instincts were too keen, and he knew her too well. With feigned nonchalance, she shrugged. "I've researched the job. An opportunity is presenting itself sooner than I'd expected, that's all."

He seemed far from reassured at her words. Setting his pen down carefully, he folded his hands on the desk and studied her. It took more effort than it should have to return his gaze. Something in that piercing midnight stare made her feel like she was fourteen again.

It was her grandmother who had introduced her to Jacques Martineux. They'd met when they'd been outwitting Germans in the Resistance and forged a friendship that had survived decades. The man had offered them unconditional help when they'd needed it most. But more important, he'd taught Juliette the skills she needed to attain the only goal she'd ever cared about.

She prided herself on being one of the top five international thieves in the world. She'd learned at the hands of a master. In his day, Jacques had been one of the top two, sharing the rewards, and the credit, for more than half of the most daring heists over a twenty-year period. His work had been the stuff of legends, though it had been years before she'd realized it.

He'd been retired when she'd met him, and she had no idea how old he was. He looked remarkably the same as he had that day ten years ago, with his long dark hair pulled back from a totally bald pate into a ponytail that hung to the middle of his back. He was no more than her own height, without a spare ounce of flesh on him. There wasn't a lock he couldn't open, a security system he couldn't evade. Besides the skills he'd imparted, he'd helped her learn to weigh the risks of the job against the benefits. At his hands she learned the value of research and planning, as well as the need for caution.

It was that caution that kept her silent now. They'd talk over the security details of a job beforehand, but she never revealed the target, never admitted to a theft. The easiest way to bring down a thief, he'd said repeatedly, was to turn their friends. It was as much for his sake as her own that she kept her intentions to herself.

These days he was known as the man to see when

one wanted to acquire necessities for a job, or the one with contacts for disbursement of property illegally acquired. The police would call him a fence. Jacques would be offended by the term, as he considered himself much more.

"So this well-researched job is coming together more rapidly than anticipated." He began clicking the gold pen in his hand, never looking away from her. "What does Pauline think of your haste?"

Juliette swallowed. "Grandmama understands the need for quick action." Or she would, she thought with a trace of guilt, if she could be told. Her grandmother was unfailingly practical. But she knew, deep inside where truth could hide, that the woman would have plenty to say about this particular change in their time line, and how it might affect the culmination of their own plans. Because it couldn't be avoided, Juliette preferred not to worry about it. Flexibility had always been her strong suit. Details of her final confrontation with Oppenheimer could shift somewhat, as long as the end result remained the same.

Striking at the man in a different way than planned could even be considered a bonus. The thought of lifting something from him that he wouldn't miss brought a slice of cold clean satisfaction. Only she would know, she and Sam, until such time as Sam used the information they found against the man. She was a woman to appreciate the subtle. Revenge, in its many varied flavors, was always satisfying. She'd react, adjust and move forward again once this was over. Once Sam was gone.

Her throat clutched, and she swallowed, forced

herself to meet Jacques's gaze. "You always said it's a foolish man who doesn't seize an opportunity."

"I also say recklessness wreaks havoc." He began tapping his pen against the list he'd been making. "You've never been reckless." His gaze bored into her, as if to ferret out the details she was withholding.

The real concern in his expression made something inside her soften. "No. I can't afford to be. I know what I'm doing." She recognized the truth in the words as she spoke them. The fact that her hand had been forced was the only real ripple in this proposition. She'd always intended to invade Oppenheimer's home. Much later. When the strategy she'd evolved had spun out in the path she'd designed. The act would be the culmination of everything that had been started all those years ago. This foray wouldn't change that. She wouldn't let it.

Jacques was, as always, unfailingly blunt. "You're radiating nervous energy. That's not like you, Juliette. Nerves get in the way of logic."

"Nerves can be useful if they're tempered with caution," she countered, turning another of his favorite sayings against him. She saw a glimmer of amusement chase across his laconic countenance. "Don't worry about me. I learned from the best."

He grunted at that, picked up his pen and started scratching on the pad again. "All the teaching in the world isn't much good if you ignore common sense."

If she hadn't been so jittery with the anxiety she'd apparently been unsuccessful at hiding, she'd have taken a moment to appreciate the fact that he worried about her, just a bit. The quality was rare enough in her life to be doubly valued. Her circle of intimates was small: her grandmother and Jacques. Where she shared friendship, and an odd sort of family with the man, he knew nothing of her past except what he'd guessed, knew nothing of what motivated her. Pauline was her only living relation, her only connection to the past. She'd lived with that knowledge for years, but it had never made her ache before. It suited her to blame that small pain on Sam Tremaine.

"You don't know how much I appreciate this, buddy."

Eyeing Sam grimly, Jones tipped his bottle of imported beer to his lips and drank. "You'd better. Do you have any idea what your sister is going to do when I get back home?"

"Kick your ass for sure," Sam replied cheerfully. It still caught him off guard, thinking of his baby sister Analiese involved with the grim-faced ex-agent seated across from him. Not just involved anymore, but actually engaged to marry. The thought should have brought a clutch of anxiety. He'd freely admit to sharing his brothers' overprotectiveness where Ana was concerned, and there wasn't a man alive who was good enough for her. But Jones came close. Damn close. They'd been friends and colleagues for years before burnout had driven the other man away from the agency. Sam knew exactly just how big a sacrifice it had taken for Jones to make the trip over here at his request.

"I'm going to let her guess your part in this mysterious trip I had to take, so you're not getting off scot-free yourself," the other man pointed out.

A bolt of real fear jarred him. Sam had faced assassins' bullets with less emotion than the thought of facing his diminutive sister's ire. "I'm banking on her to calm down a bit before I see her again."

"Yeah," Jones complained morosely. "I'm the one who's gonna get the brunt, and don't think I'll let you forget it." He laid a large manilla envelope on the table and nudged it toward his friend. "Detailed documentation on Oppenheimer's comings and goings. He's been spending time with some business acquaintances that you might find interesting. Best I can tell, he's wrapping things up in Germany for a while. He plans to head to his Austrian estate day after tomorrow with his fiancée."

Sam grunted, shaking the pages out of the envelope. "Pre-honeymoon getaway with wifey-to-be?"

"Don't know how relaxing it'll be." Jones ran his thumbnail under the label on the bottle. "Word is, he's been on a tear for the last few days, royally pissed about something."

Flipping the papers, Sam grinned. The man's temper was undoubtedly caused by Juliette's last heist. He hadn't asked why Oppenheimer regarded the necklace so highly. He'd been far more interested in what it represented to Juliette. Neither answer had been forthcoming.

"So." Jones slouched back in his chair, causing it to squeak warningly. "Gonna tell me why you can't use any agency operatives on this thing you've got going with Oppenheimer?"

Sam straightened the papers and began replacing them in the envelope. "Just being careful."

"Uh-huh. This have anything to do with Sterling's disappearance?"

The problem with tapping Jones for help, was that he knew just what questions to ask. It had taken his assistance, along with Ana's, to get Sam out of the small island country that Sterling had arranged for his burial place. Reaching for his glass of Scotch, he brought it to his lips.

Taking his silence for assent, Jones set his bottle back on the table. "I think I can figure what's going down. Not knowing the extent of Sterling's damage, you can't afford to trust many in the agency. Which means this thing isn't going by the regular channels. I just hope to God you're not playing cowboy on this thing."

Cowboy, the term for a rogue agent acting on his own without Headquarters's approval, was equal parts stupidity and dangerous. Sam wasn't stupid. "I'm not."

"I don't have to get back to the States right away. I can hang around long enough to give you a hand if you need it."

He wasn't a man for whom asking for help was easy. So it was doubly difficult to hear it offered freely from Jones. The man had left the agency after taking a bullet in the back from a fellow agent. Knowing what it cost the man made his offer doubly precious. "You've done enough. Whatever happens from here out is all mine."

Jones stared at him for a moment, before nodding slowly. "I'll stay for a few more days just in case. You can give me a call when you've finished whatever the hell you're doing." When Sam opened his mouth to protest, Jones leaned forward. "I'll stick around."

Arguing was futile. So was attempting to articulate just what the offer meant to him. Instead of trying, Sam raised his glass, waited for Jones to do the same.

"To success," he said simply. Unspoken understanding passed between the two men as crystal clinked against bottle.

"To success."

Wiping his bare chest with a towel, Sam didn't even try to keep his eyes off Juliette. It would have been futile, and he wasn't a man to deny himself simple pleasures. He'd determined that both of them could use a workout to battle the adrenaline that came hand in hand with an approaching assignment. But he couldn't possibly have known just what he was letting himself in for.

After going a couple rounds with the body bag, she'd moved on to the balance beam. He'd admired her form as she'd punched and kicked at the bag with enough force to send it swaying. But watching her on the beam made him sweat. She did a graceful handstand, turned with one quick movement of her wrists, then let her legs float downward in a skeletal defying position until they were parallel to the bar.

All the blood in his body abruptly pooled below his waist. He'd known, at least on a logical level, that her evasion of those laser beams in the museum had to have required a great deal of practice. He could never have imagined just what routine that practice would take. Damn if he was sure whether he was going to survive watching it.

Slowly Juliette raised her legs, poised, then did a quick flip around the bar, a lightning switch of hand placement and then reversed the action. After several dizzying flips, she stood upright, without swaying a fraction, and took a running start on the beam. Sam's throat closed and he took an involuntary step toward her as she dove into the air, somersaulted three times, and came to a standing halt on the mat.

It took a moment to get his voice to work again. "Showing off?"

She blew out a breath, reached over and snatched the towel from his hand. "Just warming up."

There was a thin trickle of perspiration along her throat, and the front of her short sports top was stained with moisture. He'd never found the sight in the least bit attractive before. And certainly he'd never had the urge to press a woman's hot sticky body against his own, to lick the salty traces of exertion from her skin.

A mental image of him doing just that burned a path across his mind. He had a vivid picture of their naked tangled bodies lying across a bed, flesh slick with moisture generated by another, far more pleasurable workout.

It took an incredible amount of effort to shove that thought aside, but carving it from his memory was going to take longer. "You could take that act on the road. Maybe get a new Olympic event started. B&E gymnastics."

Her teeth flashed in one of the few genuine smiles she'd ever given him. It did nothing to cool his fevered body. "I never thought of breaking and entering as a sporting event before. You may be onto something."

Breaking and entering. He seized the phrase and its accompanying implications. The only thing that had brought them together was her skill at theft. Her level of expertise at breaking the law, eluding capture, and taking whatever she wanted. What kind of woman made those kind of choices, led that kind of life? The answer seemed only too obvious.

"We'll need to leave for Austria first thing in the morning." Because it was easier to focus when he wasn't looking at her, he turned away, reached for his shirt. "We'll fly, then rent a car. You'll need a false passport. I trust that won't be a problem."

"I have several." He hadn't realized she'd moved until she was standing in front of him, regarding him speculatively. "How are you going to get one?"

"Don't worry about me." He didn't bother telling her that he had more than one identity himself. The revelation would elicit more questions, questions which he had no intentions of answering. In that area, too, they shared a similarity.

Shrugging into his shirt, he continued, "We need to talk about how we're circumventing each aspect of the security. I want to make sure you have all the materials you need before we leave."

"As if I'd start a job without being prepared."

He ignored the irritation shading her tone. "So you've compiled everything you'll need?"

Tossing the towel toward him, she stalked over to find her T-shirt. "I expect a delivery this evening."

"Okay." He crossed to where he'd left his clothes. Pulling a tattered pair of sweats over his shorts, he sat down and started putting on his shoes and socks. "What do you have planned for the guard dogs?"

"Tranquilizer darts. Don't worry," she said, when he shot her a look. "I have an extremely fast-acting tranq and I'm an excellent shot."

"Do you have two guns?"

"I don't expect to need…"

"Do you have," he interrupted, his tone firm, "two guns?"

She blew out a breath. "Yes."

"Good. Bring them both. We'll need to drag the dogs out of sight so no one sees them down."

"We'll remove the darts and let the animals sleep it off in the bushes." She took great care to educate herself about tranquilizers so the dogs would suffer no lasting effects. "They'll be up and around again in a half hour. It shouldn't take more than four minutes to deactivate the alarm to the house."

"And you propose to do that…how?"

She shot him a pointed look. "Look, Tremaine, you came to me for my expertise, remember? If you're thinking of micromanaging this job all the way through—don't."

He finished tying his shoes and barely managed stifling a grin. She didn't appear to enjoy having someone looking over her shoulder anymore than he enjoyed Miles doing the same. He could appreciate the sentiment. "Indulge me. Please." Although the plea he tacked on had no noticeable effect at softening her expression, he continued. "I was wondering about the alarm system you mentioned."

Noting the way her gaze narrowed, he threw up his hands to ward off her temper. "I'm not questioning your research." He was, in fact, risking both their lives on its accuracy. "But a wireless alarm system would have been much more effective, wouldn't it? One thing about Oppenheimer—he likes to have the best. I just can't figure why he'd go with a more traditional alarm system when he could have tied a wireless into his closed circuit TV. He's got guards stationed at those monitors, anyway."

She pulled the shirt over her head, smoothed it down over her stomach. He tried, not quite successfully, to keep his gaze on her face. "By going with a more traditional alarm system, he avoids making all his security reliant on one server. The CCTV cameras are to patrol the grounds. If the alarm were tied through that system too, an intruder would only have to disable one target to leave the grounds and house vulnerable." She reached down and grabbed a fresh towel, started dabbing at her throat. "As security goes, his is fairly tight."

"But not too tight for you."

Her eyebrows skimmed upward. "No system's invulnerable. The best an owner can do is make it as inconvenient or risky as possible."

Spoken, he mused, like the expert she was. "So what are you planning to do? Silence the annunciator? Jumper the magnetic switches?"

She stilled, the towel gripped in one hand. Regarding him speculatively, she said, "You seem to have more than a little familiarity in this area yourself. Where'd you happen to pick it up?"

He lifted a shoulder, rose to his feet. "Here and there."

"Uh-huh." His knowledge had obviously given her something to think about. It was a moment before she continued. "Actually, this system utilizes recessed switches, which would be difficult to jumper. A gaussmeter will detect the strength of the magnets in the system. From there it will be a simple task to replace the old magnet, opening a door."

He may not have the expertise of the agency's tech squad, but he had acquired a few facts along the way. A gaussmeter was wildly expensive. For the first time he fully appreciated the expense she'd spoken of earlier, both for the tools of her trade and the acquisition of the necessary intelligence. In a strictly objective way, of course.

She went on. "I plan to use magnets on two of the cameras, too. They'll scramble the reception enough to allow us over the wall undetected."

"You forget how long we're going to be inside," he reminded her. "It's only a matter of time before one of the guards monitoring the CCTV system goes to check the cameras out."

"It's a calculated risk. Ninety-eight percent of the time people will focus on trying to fix the monitors, since that's where the trouble usually occurs. Incapacitating three cameras, covering two different areas, will make it look like a reception problem."

"I think I've got a better idea." He almost smiled when he saw the warning flash in her eyes. She wasn't one to enjoy having her expertise questioned. "Just a minute. I'll show you."

He went to the laptop he'd set next to his gym bag. From the zippered side he removed the black leather pouch the tech squad had prepared at Headquarters to send with Miles. Coming back to the safe house to work out had given him a chance to retrieve them from what had, until he'd moved in with Juliette, been his bedroom.

Crossing back to her, he opened the bag and poured several small metal devices into her cupped palms. "Microsize stegometers." She was holding one close, studying it curiously. "We attach one to the side of the cameras we want out of commission about an hour before we plan to scale the walls. It stores everything the camera 'sees' during that space of time. Then when we're ready, I'll program them to replay that same hour of tape, rather than recording as usual.''

From the stunned fascination on her face, one would think she'd found the Holy Grail. ''Where did you get these?''

''I have sources of my own.'' He scooped them from her palms, not unaware of the fact that she didn't give them up quite willingly. ''And before you ask, there's no chance I'd give you one to benefit your ill-fated career.''

A pout settled on her mouth. ''I wasn't going to ask.''

Without thinking, he tapped her sulky lips. ''Yes, you were. Even now you're trying to figure out a way to sneak a couple of them away before this thing is over. Don't bother. They'll be in my possession the whole time.''

She knocked his hand away. ''You don't know me nearly as well as you think, Tremaine.'' Her gaze went to the devices, which even now were being replaced in the pouch. ''Of course, if you were to think of making a trade for one, I wouldn't be opposed.''

Contrary to her slightly teasing tone, his own was serious as he picked up the laptop and gym bag. ''The only thing I want from you, Juliette, would be worth nothing if it wasn't offered willingly.''

Awareness flooded her expression, and he turned away, already regretting the words. But he couldn't deny their truth. He just wasn't sure what the hell he was going to do about it.

Darkness held no hidden fears for Juliette. She was most comfortable shrouded in shadows. The night held doubts at bay, made the choices that guided her life seem clear and just.

She sat in the middle of her antique four-poster hugging her knees as sleep continued to elude her. It was the thought of finally entering Oppenheimer's estate, of course. Her throat dried even as she thought it. Although this wasn't the culmination of her own plans, far from it, it did mean striking where he felt safest. Least vulnerable.

Resting her chin on her knees, she considered that thought. With him in the home as they accessed the vault, she'd be closer to him than she'd been since that day ten years ago. Revulsion crawled up her spine. She could still hear his voice, still feel the weight of his body holding her pinned to the floor. Her cheek stung, as if the sensation was summoned by the recollection of his blow.

Stop your screaming, you little bitch. You're plenty old enough to learn the only damn thing women are good for.

No, doubts didn't roam at night, but memories did. And she knew from bitter past experience that, left unchecked, they could sneak past defenses, undermine purpose by eliciting a burning slash of hatred so deep it frightened even her. From long practice she slammed the mental doors on those memories, tucked them deep into the recess of her mind, where they couldn't prey on old wounds. Emotion was the enemy of purpose. Where feeling could derail logic, focus and planning would, in the end, help her achieve her goals.

She squeezed her eyes shut, began to rock. Revenge was best served cold. So the saying went. Hers had been years in the making, and through patience and skill she'd be the one to topple Hans Oppenheimer's empire. First she'd rob him of everything he prized most, one piece at a time. That step had been highly successful so far. When he least expected it, she'd strike at his reputation, shredding his chances to gain trust, to make valuable contacts. And when he was ruined, vulnerable and exposed, she'd make him pay.

Her eyes burned with tears that would never be shed. Before she was through he'd pay for everything.

Chapter 7

At any other time Juliette might have appreciated the beauty of the Austrian countryside at dusk. The flight had gone off without a hitch. She slid a glance to the man silently driving the car down the rural road. His passport had held up as well as her own, with neither of them receiving more than a cursory glance. The same could not be said about their luggage. When asked about the nature of the equipment they carried, Juliette had launched into a dry discourse on the scientific nature of the gaussmeter. By the time she'd gotten to Carl Friedrich Gauss's contribution to the area of electromagnetism, the customs agent's eyes had glazed over, and they'd been hurriedly waved through the line.

As if feeling her gaze on him, he looked over. "What?"

"Nothing." She settled back in her seat, watching the heavily forested hills go by as their car climbed higher. "Just thinking that you don't look much like a Lestor Nilson."

"And you don't much appear like a doctoral student of mathematics. Your lecture, however, was quite convincing."

Smiling smugly, she said, "Thank you. Had there been a need, I was prepared to expound on the device's usefulness in fields as diverse as aerospace to paranormal investigations."

She'd managed to capture his interest. "Ghost hunting?"

"That's right." That explanation had come in handy a time or two, as well. "It's used to seek out disruptions in the natural magnetic fields of locations."

"Whatever that means."

She lifted a shoulder. "It pays to be convincing." In Europe she often drove to the site of her targets. Much of her equipment could be stored beneath back seats, where it escaped detection altogether. It was safer to avoid any conversations that a customs agent might remember later. However, for reasons Sam refused to explain, time was of the essence for this job.

Nerves she'd never admit to twisted in her stomach. Lack of readiness wasn't the problem. They were both prepared for this mission. It was Sam's presence that elicited the unfamiliar anxiety. "How can we be assured of Oppenheimer's arrival time?" It made her jittery to leave details in someone else's hands, to give up that amount of control. It was one reason she'd always chosen to work alone. That, and the level of trust it would require to share the nature of her jobs with another was unfathomable.

"Don't worry." Sam steered the nondescript sedan into the hairpin turns expertly. "I have someone trailing him. Suitable delays will be arranged if needed."

She would have liked to question him about those delays. As a matter of fact, she had a lot of things she'd like to ask him about. What was Miles's role in this thing? Where had he gotten those state-of-the-art devices he'd shown her yesterday, and exactly what sort of information did Oppenheimer have that was so important to Sam?

Refraining from asking any of those questions removed an opportunity for him to refuse to answer, or worse, to lie. The upcoming hours would be difficult enough without more evasions between them. She was better off knowing as little about Sam Tremaine as possible. After this job was over, there should be nothing to prevent them from parting ways. The thought brought a pang.

Uncomfortable with the reaction, she shifted in the seat. It was because she'd have to leave Paris, of course. It had been the first real home she'd had since leaving the States fifteen years ago. But a new country…a new identity would be necessary, regardless of Sam's promises. Even after he handed over the file he had on her, she'd have no way of knowing if he'd made copies, or who else he might have shared the information with.

A fresh start in a new place would also ensure that he would never find her again. Never be able to threaten her with exposure again. Never take over her life for a time and change its direction. Nor chip away at those defenses she'd spent a lifetime building, one layer at a time.

She was honest enough to admit that it was the

last thought that provided the most relief. He'd gotten too close, too fast. Maybe it was because he'd taken her so by surprise the first time they'd met. She'd felt a little off-kilter ever since. Perhaps it was the thought of him making a study of her while she was still unaware of his existence. The vulnerability that came from his knowledge left her feeling jittery and exposed.

Night was falling, and with the increasing darkness came a measure of calm. The job came first with her; that much at least hadn't changed. Faced with a target and a well-researched plan, it should be simple to keep her mind on the goal. And oddly satisfying to strike again so soon at Oppenheimer, even if he wouldn't know it.

The forests on either side of the trees began to thin, and the road seemed to level out. Although Juliette had never been to this estate of Oppenheimer's, she had aerial shots of it. Situated on a heavily forested plateau, it faced a huge lake. She'd often wondered why he'd bothered paying for lakefront property. The high wall he'd built around it would hamper any view. But then, the man had always had to have the best, regardless of the cost. And he'd never spared any scruples to get it.

There was a reflection up ahead, moonlight glinting off water. Leaning forward, she took out a pair of night-vision binoculars and raised them. Scanning the distance, she could see the vast lake, and nearby, the dark walls that absorbed the mirror reflection.

"It's just ahead, maybe a couple of miles," she murmured. She lowered the glasses to look at Sam. "We'll have to ditch the car in the woods soon."

Sam nodded. "We'll carry the equipment the rest

of the way. From which direction do you want to access the grounds?''

''Southeast,'' she said without hesitation. It would be on the opposite side from the guard house, with its CCTV monitor station. ''We'll get into the house through a side door that will lead through a large living room. It's actually farther away from the office than the back door would be, but its location eliminates the chance that someone in the guard house would see us.''

''What about servants?''

This area would be trickier. ''I know their usual hours,'' she admitted, ''but there's no way of telling if Oppenheimer's arrival will vary that. There could well be more people in the house than usual, working later to ready the place for his return.'' She shrugged fatalistically.

Sam glanced at her. ''That certainly increases the risk.''

''It might. If we enter late enough, chances are they'll be gone. No servants actually sleep there, so that's in our favor. But we have to be prepared for the possibility that one or more stay to welcome him home.''

He was nodding. ''A UFC, then.''

''What?''

''An unforeseen circumstance.'' The sedan jolted as he drove off the road and up a rutted path into the darkened woods. He drove in far enough for the forest to swallow the vehicle, obscuring it from the road.

''Exactly,'' she said approvingly. Bracing one hand on the dash, she attempted to ride out the remainder of the journey without losing any of her teeth in the process. "In any job there are matters that can't be planned for. A guard changing his routine for some unknown reason, exterminators who make a call after hours."

"I imagine you've run into your share of situations like that."

His tone was even. She wondered if she was imagining the hint of censure in it. "All the time. It's just a matter of being flexible, thinking on your feet. Does the job need to be called off, or merely postponed for a few hours."

He brought the car to a halt and killed the lights. Looking across the darkened interior at her, he said flatly, "Regardless of the circumstances, this job won't be called off."

Because it wasn't worth an argument, she said nothing. Realistically, however, she knew that situations could arise that would make retreat their only option. But she was no less determined than him to see this job through. Her grandmother's impending freedom hung in the balance. And she couldn't deny her own burning desire to proceed with this. It would be a dry run, she told herself, bending forward to tuck the binoculars back in the bag. Preparation for the time when she'd confront Oppenheimer in person, and send everything he'd worked for crashing down around him. She had a feeling that hers and Sam's goals were remarkably similar in that respect.

She looked over at him, found him pulling on thin dark gloves. "Ready?"

He reached for the door handle. "I've been ready for this longer than you can imagine."

Silently, she opened her own door. She could have uttered those words herself.

The trek to the property was a little over two miles. Carrying their equipment that far made Juliette glad she engaged in regular conditioning. Upon reaching the massive wall that surrounded the estate, she shrugged out of her backpack and set it on the ground. The moon was slivered, hanging low in the sky, and Sam was only a shadow, even standing right next to her. Like her, he was dressed completely in black, much as he'd been at the museum that night. "The cameras we'll be taking out are there," she pointed almost directly overhead, "and about thirty feet down this wall to the north. Any special place on the camera that you want those devices placed?"

He was already unzipping the laptop's case and turning the machine on. "Put it on the top, center of the camera. As long as you have it secure, I should be able to manipulate it."

Nodding, she bent, unzipped her backpack. First she put on a pair of gloves, then withdrew a grappling hook with a pair of cables attached. The cameras were located every thirty feet, just to the left of the reinforced concrete posts. Tipping her head back, she studied the solid wall for a moment, then took a position a few feet away. It took three tries before she managed to secure the hook tightly to the top. She tested the cable for support, then, satisfied, let it drop and crossed back to Sam.

Pitching her voice low, she said, "I'm ready to disable the cameras. Give me the stegometers."

He was sitting cross-legged on the grass, the computer balanced on his knees. Without taking his eyes off the screen, he reached into the pack beside him and then handed her one of the devices.

Insulted, she nudged him with her foot. "What's

the matter, Tremaine? Afraid I'll run off if I get a couple of these in my possession?''

He did look up then, flashed her an easy grin. ''No use taking chances of dropping one, is there?''

Juliette glared at him, then snatched the device from his hand. She wasn't a woman to trust easily. Certainly she was wary about putting her trust in this man. So it shouldn't wound her, deep in the recesses of her heart, to discover that he felt the same way about her.

Slipping the gadget into the pouch around her middle, she reached up and pulled the dark hood over her face. Then she went to the cable, grasped it in both hands and swung her feet to plant them against the side. Nimbly, she climbed the wall until she was within a few inches of the top. Keeping one foot precariously situated against the wall to secure her position, she took the stegometer out with one hand as she raised the other, trying to find the camera on the other side by touch. When her fingers found it, she exchanged the device to the other hand and attached it to the top of the camera.

Mission accomplished, she rappelled down the cable as quickly as she'd ascended it. She rejoined Sam and peered over his shoulder. The figures on the computer screen could have been hieroglyphics for all the sense they made to her. ''Is it working?'' she murmured.

''Let's see.'' He pressed a command and waited. A moment later, a picture appeared on the screen, a view of the grounds and the darkened house. ''Yep. Like a charm.'' He checked the time in the corner of the screen and punched in some numbers. ''A half hour should be enough time, don't you think?''

''The longer you record, the more chance you have of getting something in the picture that will give it away,'' she pointed out. ''If a rabbit should happen to hop into the camera view, the guards would get suspicious to see it in exactly the same spot over and over again.''

''That's the beauty of these little babies.'' Sam reached into his bag and withdrew one more, handed it to her. ''Once we're inside the house I can use the computer to command them. When I shut them off, the cameras will function as normal. Turn them on again and the tape we're making will come on.''

A mercenary stab of envy pierced her. The mechanisms would be priceless in her line of work. With a glance at Sam's face, she had a feeling he knew exactly what she was thinking. Last night she'd been half joking when she'd mentioned working out a trade for one of the devices. His words then had been burned in her mind ever since.

The only thing I want from you, Juliette, would be worth nothing if it wasn't offered willingly.

Her cheeks burned beneath the hood. She hadn't been thinking of sex when she'd uttered the words, but she'd thought of it often since then. Sex with him. Raw and demanding. It wouldn't be quick, or easy. He wouldn't be content with a physically satisfying romp that stopped short of true intimacy. She knew that intuitively. He'd insist on delving below the surface, peeling away layers of careful defenses in search of the real woman beneath. The shudder that worked down her spine was equal parts arousal and fear. The sensations he was capable of evoking from her weren't worth the risk of being that vulnerable. She'd never willingly offer that, not to any man.

Without another word, she moved away, reattached the hook to the wall a distance away and repeated the maneuver, securing the device to the top of the camera and climbing down again. She left the hook and cables in place. They'd use both to get over the wall when the time came.

Dropping to the ground, she strolled over to where Sam was bent over the computer. "Everything okay?" she inquired, kneeling beside him.

"They're working perfectly." With nimble fingers flying over the keys, he finished typing commands, and she saw the view of the second camera fill the screen. "They're both recording. Now all we do is wait."

Patience didn't come naturally to Juliette. Because it was critical in her line of work, she'd deliberately cultivated the trait. She'd once hidden five hours inside a cold air shaft, waiting for an overly amorous guard and his paramour to finish their night of stolen passion. But somehow, with Sam Tremaine at her side, patience seemed even more elusive. The man made her edgy. She was too aware of him for it to be otherwise.

He reached into the bag on the ground next to him and took out a cell phone. Punching out a number, he spoke quietly into it for a few moments, before looking over at her. "Oppenheimer is about an hour and half from here. Is that enough time?"

"Plenty." While the cameras replayed the scenes they were recording at that moment, they'd make their move. Accessing the house shouldn't take more than fifteen minutes, tops. Then of course, their real work would begin.

Sam spoke into the phone again. "We're good to go. Thanks a lot, buddy. I owe you one." Juliette's interest sharpened. It didn't sound as though he was talking to one of the seemingly endless string of associates he had. Who was helping him then? Miles?

There was no time to ask him, because he was already making another call. "It's me." His gaze met hers. "You can let her go now."

Her eyes widened, and it was a moment before she could reach for the phone he was holding out to her. Her tone pitched to a near whisper, she said, "Grandmama?" The sound of Pauline's voice sent a tide of relief flooding through her. Very much aware of Sam's presence beside her, Juliette wasted no time instructing her grandmother to leave the city immediately. "Just take what you'll need for a few days. You know where to go."

The older woman didn't ask questions. Juliette was thankful for that, because she was unwilling to give Sam even the slightest idea of where she was sending her. He'd have her followed of course. She didn't doubt that. But she could count on Pauline to slip away from Tremaine's associates. The woman had taught Juliette a thing or two about being cautious.

Once she'd directed her grandmother to call when she reached her destination, she disconnected and handed the phone back to Sam. Her gaze searched his. "Why did you do that?"

"What?"

"Give the order to release her now. We agreed to wait until we were inside."

"It's safer out here. There's no chance of being

overheard. Besides—'' his expression was sober, certain ''—you couldn't back out now, could you Juliette? You want to get inside almost as badly as I do.''

She flinched. His words were no less than the truth, but it didn't mean she was comfortable with having that all-assessing gaze turned on her. Although he couldn't know about her past, he understood her a little too well. She could no more have turned away at this point than she could veer from the path she'd set for herself. This unexpected opportunity to strike at Oppenheimer was too rich, too delicious to pass up.

But it wasn't the thought of accessing the man's home that filled her with an inexplicable warm glow. Sam might think he knew her on some level. But to allow her grandmother's freedom before she'd gotten them inside the estate also told her that he trusted her. Just a bit.

They spoke little after that, Sam monitoring the views on the computer screen, and Juliette checking and rechecking her equipment. In the distance she could hear the sound of the gentle waves of the lake, lapping at the shore. The water, combined with the altitude, cooled the night air to an unseasonable chill. She didn't like to wear any extra layers of clothing to get in the way on a job, so she'd foregone a jacket. Sam had done the same. She was glad for her long sleeves, but the brisk air didn't seem to be bothering him. His perfect profile could have been etched in stone, an artist's rendering of a fallen archangel. She shook off the fanciful thought. Whatever had brought Sam to her, heaven had had no hand in it, that was assured.

At that moment he turned his head, caught her

gaze on him. His expression didn't change, but his eyes did. The flash of hunger in them called to an answering emotion, demanded a response.

Afraid her reaction was all too visible on her face, she reached for her pack, ducking her head as she dug for the night-vision binoculars. ''I'm going to see if anyone's coming,'' she murmured. Sam offered no protest as she rose on shaky legs and went to do a perimeter scan. She stopped short of the road that ran in front of the estate and backtracked to check out the opposite side of the compound. Oppenheimer had cameras mounted beside the gates blocking his driveway, and she didn't know their range. There had been no reason to find out. She would never have contemplated going through the front. The risk was too great.

There was no activity either on the road or around the compound. She hadn't expected any. It was nearly ten-thirty. The guard rotation should have taken place a half hour earlier. She'd heard the dogs barking as the shift change had occurred. It had been another reason to pick the time they recorded very carefully. The comings and goings would have kept the dogs busy near the drive or guard station. They wouldn't be likely to wander near enough to be recorded, making an alert guard wonder why he was seeing three or four dogs on the combined screens instead of two.

When she made her way back to where Sam was hidden, he looked up and asked, ''All clear?'' When she nodded, he said, ''It's nearly time. We'd better get ready.'' Juliette shrugged into her backpack. With the equipment inside, it weighed nearly fifty pounds. She was glad she wasn't going to have to carry it far.

Sam shut down the computer and tucked it way back in its carrying case. Slinging the long strap over one shoulder, he slipped the handle of his other bag over his head. "I'll take one of those," he said, as she was snugging a tranquilizer gun into her waistband.

She didn't waste time arguing. He'd been adamant about it the last time they'd spoken. Slapping the extra gun in his hand, she searched in her bag and came up with three one-CC darts, each with safety tips on them. "Try not to shoot yourself, or worse, me. I carry an antidote but administering it will slow us down a bit."

He hefted the air pistol, took imaginary aim at the wall before him. "What's its range?"

"I believe there's a saying in your country." She waited for his brows to rise quizzically before continuing. "Don't shoot until you see the whites of their eyes."

"Or in this case, their fangs," he muttered.

Apprehension snuck in, and she frowned at him. "You can shoot, can't you?"

"Don't worry about me." After checking for the safety, he shoved the gun into the waistband of his pants. "I grew up with guns."

"These pistols aren't fancy, just point and fire. It's important to reload quickly, in case the dog keeps coming."

They both went to the cable. When she looked at him, he made a sweeping gesture with one hand. "After you." Reaching for her hood, she pulled it down over her face and adjusted it so she could see clearly. Grasping the rope in both hands, she gave a little hop, bracing her feet against the wall. As she walked rapidly up it, she allowed herself only one look down.

Sure enough, Tremaine was standing directly beneath her with his head tilted back, looking for all the world like a man who appreciated the view. Juliette resolved to give him a good push later.

She tossed the second cable attached to the hook down the other side of the wall and descended. While she was waiting for Sam, she kept a careful eye out for the dogs. Neither were in sight.

Moments later, Sam was dropping lightly to the ground beside her. "Any sign of them?"

Juliette shook her head and started across the lawn. "Sometimes you get lucky." It was a good eighth of a mile across the grass to the house. She and Sam jogged the distance silently. She was already planning the next step of the plan, that of entering the house. Once inside they'd have to take extra care not to cross paths with anyone. And there was still a need to find a place to hide out while waiting for this job to go down. She wished, not for the first time, that the time she was going to spend waiting wasn't going to be done with Sam by her side.

The dogs came out of nowhere. They'd no sooner stepped onto the terrace outside the door they'd access than Juliette heard a warning growl to the left of her. Swinging toward that direction, she raised her gun, calmly waited for the animal to draw nearer, then shot. The dog staggered, stopped, and she swung around while reloading. There was no need. He'd already dropped that dog.

She was in the middle of turning back to the first

animal when she heard a low growl again, slower, but infinitely dangerous. Her eyes widened as Sam uttered a curse. The first dog drew back on its haunches, then launched itself at her like a canine missile, its gaping jaws snapping at her throat.

Chapter 8

Juliette backpedaled furiously, and raised her reloaded tranquilizer gun. But before her finger reached the trigger, another dart hit the dog in the chest and it stumbled, before dropping to lie at her feet. She stared at it for a second, still picturing the razor-sharp fangs that had gotten just a little too close for comfort.

"Second gun came in handy, huh?"

She looked up at Sam, attempting to shift her attention back to the job. "Yeah." She cleared her throat. "I guess so." He bent to retrieve the darts, and his action shook her out of her unusual abstraction. "Be careful with them," she breathed. "Here." She pulled out a Ziploc bag filled with cotton batting and held it open for him to place them inside. When he'd removed all three darts from the animals, she cautiously rolled them up in the baggie and put it in the leather pouch at her waist. She let Sam carry the dogs to some nearby bushes while she crossed to the door they'd access. Letting the backpack slide down her arms, she set it on the ground near her feet, bent, and started taking out the equipment she'd need.

She shone a penlight on the door, didn't see a magnetic contact. Even if she hadn't paid for top of the line intelligence on Oppenheimer's security system, she wouldn't have been fooled into thinking the door was unprotected. More and more security companies were using recessed switches, with the magnet placed in the door, and the switch someplace in the door frame.

Like a surgeon laying out his instruments, Juliette lined up the equipment she'd need for this stage of the job. She picked up the liquid-filled compass and began to pass it slowly around the edge of the door. When she reached a point where it reacted wildly, she knew she'd found the magnet.

Sam's voice breathed in her ear, "Want me to hold the flashlight?"

"No, but you can hold this. Right where it is." She waited until he'd taken the compass and held it positioned correctly before reaching for the gaussmeter. She stood, nudged him aside and held the instrument to the place where the compass had reacted. Studying the face of the gaussmeter, she quickly figured the exact magnetic strength of magnet used to close the switch.

She bent down over her bag again, this time to replace the gadget and hunt for the box of magnets she'd packed. Selecting two with the same strength as the one detected in the door, she slipped one into her pocket and then rose. Stepping around Sam, she held the other to the spot where the magnet was recessed.

Juliette breathed out a sigh of satisfaction when she felt the powerful magnetic pull. ''Hand me that packet of picks, will you?'' He went down on one knee near the equipment she'd laid out and silently held them up for her perusal. She selected the tool she wanted, and went to work on the door's lock. Twenty seconds later, she felt it give, and she silently berated herself. It should have taken her no more than ten. She needed practice.

Dropping the pick into the packet Sam still held, she took another and went to work on the dead bolt. It opened in record time, partially easing her earlier dismay.

''Wire,'' she whispered, and Sam held up the thin metal length she'd laid out. She exchanged it for the discarded pick and took a moment to haul in a breath. She affixed the magnet to the wire, and then fed the end into the door as she reached for the knob. Slowly, keeping her gaze on the position of the magnet, she opened the door a fraction at a time, feeding the magnet and wire in to circumvent the switch.

The door opened, she looked back at Sam, but he'd read her mind and had already packed all her tools back in her bag. Rising, he nodded and she turned, taking the extra magnet out of her pocket as she maintained her grasp on the wire. Slipping inside, she held the second magnet to the other side of the door, signaled to Sam to grab the wire and outside magnet, then gestured for him to join her. Closing the door behind him, she retrieved her second magnet and consulted her watch. The whole operation had taken less than ten minutes.

She looked at Sam. His hood was nearly identical to hers, obscuring his face completely. No one would ever have been fooled by the color of those eyes, though. And right now they were glinting at her in amusement.

His voice near silent, he whispered, "Nice. But we're not done yet, so don't get cocky."

Her narrowed glare should have said it all. And maybe it did, because when she grabbed her bag from him and turned, she felt an unmistakable pinch on her bottom. Resisting the urge to drive her elbow into his stomach, she made a mental note to pay him back later. When they were safely out of here with the information he wanted.

The interior of the house was shadowy and quiet except for the ticking of an unseen clock. With her index finger raised to her lips, she gestured for Sam to follow her as she crossed the large living room and pressed herself to a wall next to the door exiting into a large hallway. Craning her neck, she could see a dim light. She mentally visualized the house blueprint in her head. The light would be coming from the kitchen. Which meant all the servants hadn't yet left.

Ducking back inside the living room, she pressed her mouth to Sam's ear to whisper, "Someone's here. I'm going to check it out."

His hand snapped around her wrist, halting her. "Maybe we should wait," he breathed. "We've got some time."

Juliette shook her head impatiently. "They could be planning to stay until he gets home. Let me go. I'll be right back."

It took a moment before his grip loosened. Another before she could tug free. Obviously he still had reservations, but she wasn't going to stick around and discuss them further. He'd hired her for her expertise and judgment. Evaluating the ongoing risks was just part of the job.

She tiptoed into the hallway and pressed herself against the opposite wall. Keeping in the shadows, she sidled closer to the light, until she could hear the sound of voices. She stilled, listened. When she could make out the words she moved a little closer.

German. Upon identifying the language the speaker was using she realized something else. It was only one voice, speaking, stopping, speaking again. Talking on the phone.

"Ich warte Ihre Ankunft." Silence. Then, *"Ja Sir. Alles ist zu Ihnen bereit."* Pause. *"Wie Sie wünschen."* Juliette heard the sound of the receiver being replaced in the cradle. A few minutes later the kitchen light switched off, and there was the sound of a door opening then closing again. She made her way back to the living room. It was hard to distinguish Sam from the shadows. When she did get close enough to make out his form, an involuntary gasp escaped her when she saw the snub-nosed revolver grasped in his hand.

"What are you doing?" It took more effort than it should have to keep her voice pitched to a whisper. She never carried guns on a job, although she knew how to handle one. She fully ascribed to Jacques's theory that a good thief needed to rely on wits, research and cunning to make an escape. Guns should only be carried by people who had every intention of using them. It didn't make her feel any better to note that Sam looked as though he was capable of doing that very thing.

"Put it away," she commanded. He lowered the gun, but didn't comply.

"What'd you find out?"

With one last glance at the weapon in his hand, she whispered, "There was one person in the kitchen. Probably the housekeeper or cook. I think she just got off the phone with Oppenheimer. He told her to go home. She just left."

"Anyone else in the house?"

"There doesn't appear to be anyone downstairs, at least. No other lights are on."

"Ready to move, then?"

"Not until you put that gun away." Her tone was adamant. His response was equally so.

"No."

She restrained the urge to kick him in his bad leg again. "I've never taken a gun with me on a job, and I don't intend to start now."

"You didn't. I did."

There was something decidedly unsatisfying about holding an argument in whispers. Her curse, however, was no less vehement for its lack of volume. *"Damnez-vous à l'enfer et au dos!"*

"Have you ever seen the remains of someone who's crossed Oppenheimer?" Something in his near silent voice halted her own. "I have. The man is merciless, and he takes delight in inflicting the greatest amount of pain before death. If you think I'm going to let either of us take this kind of chance without some sort of defense, you're not as intelligent as I give you credit for."

She'd never seen his eyes look that cold, that flat.

His words summoned a brief visual memory that was better left tucked away. Juliette knew firsthand just what kind of sadistic monster Oppenheimer was. One of the driving forces in her life was her vow that she was never going to be helpless around the man again.

The rest of her protest slid down her throat, unuttered. With a curt nod, she picked up her pack and walked by him, her steps noiseless. He was just as quiet when he followed. But his reminder of the danger of this mission lingered between them. Juliette knew that if Oppenheimer ever caught her, she'd pray for death long before it was delivered. And if he discovered her identity, he'd make sure she suffered tremendously before killing her.

She banished the chill that accompanied the thought by stiffening her spine. She'd successfully avoided capture for ten years, her eye on one goal—bringing down Oppenheimer. No one could match her for motivation. And she wasn't going to get caught this time. Not when it would risk everything she'd worked for. Not when it would bring an early end to her quest for revenge.

Leading Sam down the darkened hallway, she went unerringly to the study. The door was closed, and she tried the handle. Locked. The schematics she'd acquired didn't mention any security protecting this entrance, but she reached into her bag anyway, and pulled out a thin metal wand. Clicking it on, she ran it along the door frame, over the door itself, checking for electrical impulses that would be evidence of some sort of protection. Nothing registered on the wand; its light remained dim. Content that her intelligence had been correct, she set it down, took out a pick and had the door open in moments. Before she walked through it, she waved the wand inside the narrow opening. The screen showed no evidence of security measures inside either, so she went inside. Once Sam was beside her, she shut the door and relocked it.

"We've got about forty-five minutes left."

Nodding she said, "See if you can find a place in here for us to hide. It would be easiest if we could stay in this room while we wait." Leaving him to look around, she went unerringly to what appeared to be a closet door in the corner of the room. But it was far more than that, she knew. It was the entry to the vault, which held the information Sam sought.

She took out the bottle of ultraviolet ink and painted the doorknob with the substance. Odorless and colorless, it would be undetectable to the naked eye. When she finished, she replaced the cap on the bottle and turned to see what Sam had discovered.

With a sound of disgust, she found him sitting in back of Oppenheimer's desk, rifling through the contents of a drawer. Juliette crossed to him. "Those had to have been locked."

He didn't bother looking up. "You're not the only one with hidden talents." Obviously finding the papers of no interest, he put them away and relocked the drawer. As he bent over the next one, she noted he was using a pick from her own set.

Irritation surged. "Give me that."

He looked up as she made a grab for it. Teeth gleaming behind the black mask, he held it out of her reach. "I'm going to put it back. Don't be selfish. Didn't you ever learn to share?"

It did nothing to douse her annoyance when he opened the next drawer with little effort. As she'd noted before, the man had more than a few illegal skills himself. "I flunked playing nice in kindergarten. The last little boy to use something of mine without permission got a Tonka truck alongside his head."

Maddeningly, he grinned. Having scanned the documents in that drawer and obviously not finding them important, he put them back and secured the lock. "Ah, so you *are* from the States."

Juliette froze, unable to believe what she'd just said. Not that the information was critical, but she'd never given away any information about her past, not even something as insignificant as this. It was one more piece of evidence that Sam was getting too close. He was sneaking through defenses she'd once sworn were impenetrable. Getting closer to her than any man had ever been.

That thought alone was enough to send terror streaking up her spine. She clutched the edge of the desk with her gloved fingertips. It didn't matter, she assured herself frantically, ignoring the mocking voice deep inside that called her a liar. This would be over soon, and then Sam would be gone. She clung to that thought. And when it was, no one else would get this near. No one else would *know* so much about her. Small bits of knowledge, every one, but taken as a whole they painted a picture that was too accurate for her peace of mind. Juliette was comfortable living illusions of her own creation. There was no room in her life for a man intent on stripping them away, piece by piece.

He finished with the last drawer and checked his watch again. "Now, you were saying…a place to hide.'' He swept the room with his gaze, then looked back at her and pointed. ''How about in there?''

When she saw where he was pointing, dismay filled her. But he was already crossing the room toward the antique cabinet sitting in one corner of the room. It looked to be Asian in origin, handpainted with pictures and symbols which would tell something of its history. But for once the beauty and obvious value of a piece was lost on her. Her attention was focused on its size.

It was narrow, barely three feet wide, and would require them to be pressed closely together for the entire time. Juliette's breath trapped in her lungs at the very thought. They would most likely be waiting for hours; longer if Oppenheimer didn't go to the vault until tomorrow. There was no way she could survive spending that much time pressed up against Sam Tremaine. Every nerve in her body quivered at the thought.

He opened it, made a sound of disappointment. ''It has shelves.'' He pulled testingly at the edges of a couple, before closing the door and turning toward her. ''They're not removable.''

''Too bad,'' she whispered back, secretly awash in relief. She took out her flashlight, and, being careful to shield the beam with her hands, sent it sweeping across the room. It quickly became apparent that their options in this room were depressingly limited. Besides the desk, there was a couch, some chairs and a modern entertainment center holding a big-screen TV. Rare and unusual objects of art were displayed, from ancient African pottery to a framed Rembrandt whose authenticity she didn't doubt. But there was no place that would afford them a place to hide and escape detection.

Philosophically, she shrugged when Sam looked at her. "We'll have to find somewhere else."

"Where?"

She noted, almost absently, that he was rubbing his injured thigh. With their exertions of the evening, it had to be sore from the strain. "Outside the room. Maybe somewhere in the hallway." She was halfway to the door before she realized he wasn't by her side. Turning, she found him taking something from the bag he carried.

Instantly suspicious, she retraced her steps. "What's that?"

"A little insurance." He went behind the desk again, this time dropping to his hands and knees.

Curious and more than a little wary, she trailed behind him to watch him affix something to the mop board. Squatting beside him, she shone her flashlight on what looked like a small nail head. "What is it? Why do you…" Comprehension registered. "Oh, no."

His eyes met hers. "Oh, yes."

"Absolutely not," she said in a furious whisper. It was easy to see that she'd neglected to make some things very clear before they'd set out for this job. "We're not planting a bug. He's sure to use detectors, and it's not worth the risk. He's traveling only with his fiancée, so you're not likely to pick up any meaningful conversation anyway."

"Don't worry." He rose, dusted off his pants. "This device doesn't cause voltage to fluctuate, so it can't be picked up by an oscilloscope."

"What about a metal detector?" she demanded.

His shrug was too nonchalant. "It does well with them too."

"How well?"

"Avoids detection seventy percent of the time due to the high levels of plastic and ceramic in its makeup."

"That's not good enough!" The merits of working alone had never seemed clearer. She was comfortable weighing the risks of a job, adjusting to them accordingly. It was quite different to have a partner who escalated the danger without even running it by her first.

"Actually, it's very good. And in this case, well worth the slight gamble we'll be taking."

She struggled to keep her clenched fists at her side. "You don't get to make that decision."

His tone was even as he brushed by her to start for the door. "Lucky you're self-employed. You don't take direction worth a damn."

Perhaps he was right. Juliette hauled in a deep breath and attempted to calm the fury pumping through her veins. No other man had been able to draw this level of emotion from her. In the dim recesses of her mind she realized the significance of that fact. But of primary importance right now was that Sam didn't botch this for both of them. She knew too well that one little underestimation of risk could sink them both.

One moment she was reaching for the bug he'd planted, and the next he was behind her, his hands on her shoulders, pulling her against him. "Don't." Even at a whisper the word was laden with warning. Looking up at him she recognized the steely intent in his eyes. And knew in that instant she wasn't going to win this battle. It was dangerous to forget the air of menace the man was capable of radiating, the steely resolve. One could be fooled by his affable charm if they didn't see just this look in his eyes. A look that reminded that this was a man who'd do whatever it took to get exactly what he wanted.

His hands turned caressing on her shoulders. Kneading them gently, he murmured, ''Trust me on this. I know what I'm doing.''

The temptation to lean into that touch, into that vow, was nearly overwhelming for an instant. She actually felt her body sway toward his, as the promise in his hands and voice worked a wicked kind of magic. Then she stiffened, shrugging away from him as she rose. Juliette Morrow didn't lean. Ever. And she never, ever trusted.

Without another word she stalked toward the door, and snapped off the flashlight before she opened it. Peering out, she noted nothing out of the ordinary and widened the expanse, leaving him to trail behind her.

The foyer had an air of opulence that was apparent even in the dark. There were two closets, and silently she checked out both of them. One held coats and hangers. This door she closed. It was too likely that Oppenheimer or his fiancée would have reason to use that closet. The other was across the hall, and seemed perfect when she first opened the door. It held only a vacuum and cleaning supplies. It was highly unlikely that their quarry would be checking in here tonight, although if they had to stay beyond the night they would need to find a new hiding place before morning.

There was a glow in the dark next to her. Sam was

checking his watch. "This'll do." With a hand at her back he gave her a nudge inside, stepping in after her and pulling the door shut.

Instantly the area shrunk. The space was bigger than the cabinet he'd looked at, but not by much. Turning on her flashlight again, she attempted to re-arrange the contents of the space noiselessly. With their bags on the floor in front of them, there was barely enough room for them to sit against the back wall. When both of them did so, their shoulders, sides and legs were pressed tightly against each other.

With no little difficulty, she reached into the pouch at her waist and withdrew a paperclip. Pulling it apart, she twisted it a couple times and slipped it into the keyhole on the doorknob. She left a length pro-truding toward them so she could remove it when they were ready to move. As a deterrent, it wasn't much, but it would jam the door long enough for them to prepare themselves.

Sam snatched the flashlight from her and used it as he opened the laptop, tapped in the commands that would allow the cameras to return to their original function. In the light afforded from the screen, she was able to make out a dark earpiece he wore. The monitor for the bug they'd argued over.

Through her lingering resentment, she began to wonder about the explanation he'd given of the de-vice. Even given her experiences of the last decade, she'd never heard a listening mechanism made of plastic and ceramic. She'd used bugs herself, as a way to gain valuable information. Bank account numbers, security codes...although she'd never dared use one with Oppenheimer directly, there were other entities he dealt with that didn't have the level of security he demanded for himself. Jacques prided himself on having the most up-to-date equipment the black market had to offer, and that was usually years ahead of when it was available retail.

But Jacques had never mentioned anything like this before. For that matter, Juliette thought as she squirmed into a more comfortable position, he'd never mentioned stegometers. If they were available anywhere, he'd know about them. Which meant Sam's possession of these state-of-the-art devices was more than a little thought-provoking.

Whatever Sam Tremaine was, she decided, he wasn't a businessman out to steal rival secrets from Hans Oppenheimer. She swallowed hard at the realization, but there was no denying it. The man, who was even now pressed closer to her than any male had been in a very long time, was completely shrouded in mystery. And that thought was going to make the next few hours in this tiny area with him seem very long indeed.

Chapter 9

"Someone's coming."

Sam's voice was near soundless in her ear. Juliette nodded. She'd heard the telltale noises, too. Hardly daring to breathe, she listened as the front door was opened, and voices filled the foyer.

"Finally." The querulous tones of a woman could be heard. "Honestly, Hans, the delays on this trip were absolutely beastly. I thought we'd never get here."

"Relax, Moira, we're here now. And we have the next week to relax."

Every organ in Juliette's body seemed to freeze. Breathing stopped. Veins clogged. She hadn't heard that voice for ten years, except in the memories that wouldn't be restrained. But recognition was immediate. It summoned a violent rush of emotion that hammered through her body and left her weak.

His genial tones were less recognizable. Dimly,

she remembered a time at the beginning when he'd seemed polite, even kind. That contrast had made it even more terrifying when the mask of civility had been discarded to reveal the monster beneath.

You're nothing but a whore, do you understand that? And you're my whore…mine. For as long as I want you. The horrible rhythmic sound of a hand striking flesh melded with the voice from the past, for an instant making past and present a dizzying unidentifiable blend. A shudder worked through her, and Juliette screwed her eyes shut, beat the recollections back.

When an arm went around her, pulled her closer, she jerked, every muscle in her body going tense. Eyes flying open, her gaze met Sam's in the darkness. There was a sympathy in his that she wanted to reject, and an understanding that was all too tempting to accept. The human contact he provided was the link she needed to pull her firmly back into the present. And for a moment, just one, she sagged against him, tamping down the grief, fury and hatred. When she straightened, already embarrassed by her lapse, the memories were, if not banished, at least shaved back to the shadowy corner of her mind where they usually lurked.

''I sent the servants home, but there should be a meal prepared for us to heat up.'' A door opened, and after a few moments, closed again. Juliette was thankful they hadn't elected to wait in the coat closet. Even if they had managed to avoid detection, it would have been harrowing to be that close to Oppenheimer. Revulsion crawled over her skin. Close enough to smell his cologne. To hear his breathing. Close enough to reach out and touch the man.

Heat began to chug through her veins, dissipating the earlier ice. The time would soon come when she'd be exactly that near the man. But it would be *her* time. Of *her* choosing. And when she walked away, she wouldn't be the one rendered impotent by helpless rage. That was the vow that had kept her sane for the past decade. And it calmed her now, allowed resolve to replace emotion.

Distantly, she could hear the voices fade as Oppenheimer and his fiancée moved away. She looked down, tapped her watch to illuminate its face—eleven o'clock. It would be hours before they could make their move. She tried to wedge a fraction of space between her and Sam and prepared to wait.

The hours ticked by one infinitesimal second at a time. Juliette had once perched on a four-inch cement window ledge outside a London auction house in midwinter for three hours waiting for her chance at entry. That experience had been a breeze compared to this one. At least on that ledge, she'd been *alone*.

For the tenth time in as many minutes she shifted, only to find herself pressed just as closely to Sam as she'd been the moment before. Giving up, she slumped back against the wall.

"You okay?"

Sam's lips were close enough to brush against her ear as he breathed the words. They'd both long since abandoned their hoods. The closeness of their quarters made it uncomfortably warm. Or maybe, she thought, as a shiver of awareness skated down her spine, the man at her side bore full responsibility for that.

Irritated by the involuntary response, she gave a

jerky nod. Had the closet been empty, it would have afforded them more than enough room. But one wall was filled by mops, buckets and brooms, with a vacuum tucked in the corner. The opposite wall had floor-to-ceiling shelves, stocked with cleaning supplies. That left the wall they leaned against, facing the door. With their knees drawn up and their packs beside them, there wasn't an inch to spare.

She shot him a glance. Given the width of his shoulders, he took up more than his share of space. Gave off more than his share of heat. Usually she would use this time to go over the necessary steps of the job, practicing them in her mind the way she physically practiced before setting out. But it was difficult to maintain her concentration when she was practically on Sam's lap.

"He's entered the office."

Juliette straightened at Sam's words, swiveling her head to face him, as if the position would afford her the opportunity to hear what he did. His head was slightly lowered, as he listened intently to the sounds coming through the earpiece he wore.

"Is he alone?"

Sam lifted a shoulder. It rubbed along her own. "No voices. Maybe." Several minutes passed. "He's unlocking something."

The back of her nape prickled with nerves, but she beat back the bud of anticipation that unfurled. He could be merely opening the desk drawers. They'd known from the beginning that they might have to hide somewhere in the house for a day or more while they waited for Oppenheimer to access the vault. She'd thought at the time the biggest problems with that scenario would be finding a way to relieve themselves without risking detection. That was the least of her worries now.

He reached up to adjust the earpiece, and his elbow rubbed against her breast. Despite the current of pleasure that frissoned down her spine, or perhaps because of it, she sent a not quite accidental elbow to his ribs. His injured glance didn't sway her in the least. Their close quarters meant they had to take more care than usual. It didn't hurt to remind him of that.

It took fierce physical effort to avoid squirming to a new position. It would be futile at any rate. They were seamed together, from shoulder to ankles, a length of heat pulsing between them. There had never been a job that she'd rejected based on its difficulty. There was a way to circumvent any obstacle. But right now she genuinely doubted her ability to spend a day or more cooped up with Sam Tremaine plastered against her. And if that made her weak, so be it. She doubted there was a woman alive who could ignore such a blatantly masculine male when he'd spent hours draped against her. She was just going to pray that she had only hours more to endure the torture, and not days.

Sam made a sound of disgust. She looked at him. "What?"

"He's watching a movie. Definitely X-rated. Pervert. I'd heard he started out in the porn field. Maybe it's some of his own work."

Her throat abruptly dried. She could feel the nasty little memory fragments slipping around the edges of her mind, waiting for a chance to pounce. From long habit, she firmly pushed them away. Wallowing in old fears had never changed a thing. The only thing

Oppenheimer had ever understood was action. She seized on that truth and focused on it.

If he was watching a skin flick, where had he gotten it? They'd seen no movie cases in his desk, nor on the shelves. None had been apparent in the cabinet Sam had first suggested they hide in. He wouldn't keep them out in plain view, at any rate, would he? It seemed equally odd that he would keep them in the highly secured vault.

She stole a glance at Sam. His gaze was on her. The intensity in his expression made her stomach do a neat flip. And she knew, indisputably, that the torturous awareness she'd been experiencing hadn't been one-sided. Not at all. Somehow she didn't think the knowledge would make the upcoming hours pass any more quickly.

The house had been still for well over an hour. Juliette nudged Sam, tapped her watch. He nodded, then rose, with no little difficulty, to his feet. She took the hand he extended and he pulled her up. Their proximity had her sliding along his body every inch of her ascent. If she'd had a nerve ending that wasn't already honed to rapier sharpness where he was concerned, that last move would have done it. Avoiding his gaze, she turned toward the door, gritting her teeth when her hip grazed his thigh.

Her fingers were clumsier than usual. It took longer than it should have to shine the flashlight at the doorknob, and remove the wire she'd inserted in the lock. Carefully she slipped it back into the pouch at her waist, donned her hood, and inched the door open, all too aware of the masculine body pressed firmly to her backside.

As soon as she entered the darkened silent hall-way, she filled her lungs gratefully. She took the bag Sam handed her, shrugged into it, and waited for him to pick up his own. Then, shutting the closet door behind them, they crept toward the office.

There was a narrow shaft of light showing beneath the doorway. She tugged at Sam's sleeve, pointed to it. He tapped the earpiece he still wore and shook his head. Bending his head close to hers, he whispered, "Heard him leave an hour ago. It's empty." However reassuring his words were, caution was too in-grained for her to take them at face value. She removed a slim piece of metal and began unfolding it at its joints. Going on her hands and knees, she fed one end under the door. She pressed a button that would raise the tiny lens on either end. Peering closely into the lens on her side, she manipulated the scope until she got a clear view of all angles inside the room. Sam was right. It was empty.

Ignoring the impatience evident in his posture, she checked again for security devices. Although they hadn't detected one the first time they'd entered, that didn't mean Oppenheimer hadn't activated one be-fore exiting the study. Finding none, she took out the pick, had the lock open in thirty seconds. They slipped inside, relocked the door.

Quickly they crossed to the door tucked in the cor-ner. She sprang the lock in record time, then replaced the pick in her pouch. Taking the bag off her back, she unzipped it, reached inside, withdrew a battery-operated handheld ultraviolet light. Careful to shield its glare, she clicked it on, shining its beam on the keypad to the vault.

Four of the keys shone brightly in the glare. Four-nine-six-two. A jubilant hiss came from Sam, and Juliette released the breath she hadn't realized she'd been holding. Snapping off the light, she replaced it in the backpack. Taking out a sheaf of paper, she began scanning it. The computer-generated matches with only three number sequences could be discarded. She'd start with the four-digit sequences and if that failed to garner a match, she'd try the five-digit ones.

The first combination of numbers failed. Undeterred, Juliette tried the second. Then the third. Her palms began to sweat inside the thin leather gloves she wore. However, her hands remained steady as she tried the fourth set of numbers. Then the fifth.

It wasn't until she'd keyed in the sixth sequence that the red light on the keypad blinked, a steady beacon heralding success. Reaching out, she turned the knob of the vault door, pulled it open.

Although there were precautions to take—the ink needed to be wiped off the door handle and keypad—she couldn't resist taking a look inside the vault first. It was far larger than the closet they'd taken shelter in. About twelve feet deep and at least ten wide, it had thick reinforced steel surrounding all sides. Shelving lined one wall, filing cabinets another. While she looked on, Sam went to the first of them. "Give me your pick set, will you?"

She took it from her bag and handed it to him, pausing to watch for a moment. He selected one from the set and with a few deft movements, had the drawer unlocked. She left him to rifle through it and went back to wipe away the ink. When she came back, he was already on the next file cabinet, rapidly flipping through the contents.

It looked as though he knew exactly what he was searching for. The thought occurred, and Juliette watched him more closely. Occasionally he'd pause to look more carefully at the contents of a folder, before shutting it and moving on to another. Not for the first time, she found herself wondering about his motives. What information was he after and what action would he take against Oppenheimer once he discovered it?

Those questions, though, faded in significance for the moment. Walking deeper into the vault, she noted one shelf full of DVD cases. Looking at a few, she found that each case bore a woman's name. With a shudder of revulsion, she replaced them. No doubt this was the porn collection Sam had referred to. Perhaps Oppenheimer kept them locked up to keep his fiancée in the dark about his tastes. An unfamiliar stab of pity for the woman pierced her. If the man ran true to form, she'd find out all too soon just what sort of demon he really was.

There were several jewel cases on the shelves, and Juliette opened each of them. There was an antique diamond-encrusted broach, an emerald ring easily worth a hundred grand, a necklace with a center sapphire as big around as a baby's fist. Brows skimming upward, she made a mental note of the contents. Her next foray into the man's estate wouldn't be a soft access, and he'd definitely know someone had been there once she cleaned him out of all these valuables. The thought was guaranteed to satisfy.

Moving on, she found a large square lockbox on the bottom shelf. A quick glance found Sam intently perusing some papers in a file. While she watched he took a small machine from his pack, unfolded it and pressed a button. With its power on, he ran the screen over each of the pages in turn.

For an instant she forgot the lockbox. The machine appeared to be a miniature scanner of some sort. But it was impossible to tell if it merely took pictures of the pages or was capable of transmitting them to another source. It was on the tip of her tongue to ask. In the next instant the urge died. There was a great deal Sam Tremaine hadn't told her about this job. There was no reason to think he'd tell her more now. But pieces were starting to shift into place for her. She just wasn't certain yet about the resulting picture.

He still had her pick set. She rummaged in her pouch and found the paper clip with which she'd jammed the closet door. With a few twists, she'd fashioned a pick, and wielded it on the lockbox. A few quick motions and the lock popped open.

Cautiously, she positioned herself so Sam wouldn't see what she was up to. She opened the box's lid, and then stopped, stunned.

It was filled with gold coins.

She reached for one, and upon closer examination revised her first impression. Not just coins, these were gold ingots. Undeniably old, they'd be worth a minimum of thirty thousand a piece. And there were hundreds of them in the box.

''What's in there?''

Sam's whisper had her jerking around, her fist closing around the coin she'd been looking at. Before she could answer, he got a look himself and gave a near soundless whistle. ''Quite the collector, isn't he?''

''He is, yes,'' she replied slowly. ''But he likes

the world to know what he has. That's why he loans his art to museums, puts his jewelry and ancient weaponry on display. Better than the owning, for him, is having people see what he can afford.''

His gaze met hers. ''But these have never been on display, have they?''

Juliette shook her head. It was her business to know such things. She was almost as familiar with the man's belongings as he was himself. And she'd never heard about him owning a large set of gold ingots.

As a matter of fact, she didn't remember that sapphire ever being mentioned, either. She couldn't swear about the other pieces he kept here, but she'd remember the sapphire because of its size.

''Maybe he keeps things here that he wants to protect from *le petit voleur,*'' Sam said, his voice teasing.

''I doubt it.'' She scanned the contents of the vault one more time. ''He'd consider that giving in, somehow. Agreeing that a thief could outwit him is totally against his nature. No, I think the things he keeps here are items no one can know he has.'' She met Sam's gaze. ''They're stolen.''

''Probably.''

The idea didn't seem to affect Sam one way or another. For the first time she realized the filing cabinet drawers were all shut and locked again. ''Did you find what you were looking for?''

''I think so. I'm ready to move out. Lock up that box again and be sure that everything is back in its place.''

She didn't know what made her do it. She'd never been a creature of impulse. But when she secured the lockbox she did so without replacing the ingot. That was slipped into her pocket when Sam wasn't looking.

A set of ancient ingots didn't go missing in the artifact world without eliciting some sort of talk. As Juliette followed Sam out of the vault and secured it again, she vowed to discover just what that talk was. She had many things planned for Hans Oppenheimer. If she could arrange proof that he harbored stolen property, it would be one more nail in his coffin. The thought brought a grim smile.

Sam removed the bug he'd placed in the office earlier, and they moved silently out of the room, locking it behind them. The house was still quiet when they made their way to the side door again. Pausing there, she waited for Sam to take out the laptop, turn it on and type in the command to reactivate the phony camera scans he'd programmed earlier. It didn't escape her notice that he'd also withdrawn the gun again, and had it tucked in his waistband at the base of his back. Although the sight didn't set any better with her this time, she knew better than to say something. Instead she withdrew the tranq guns. Loading each with a dart, she handed one to him and shoved hers in her waistband.

Several moments later, Sam said, "Okay. We're good to go." As he folded up the computer, Juliette took the night-vision binoculars from her pack, and slipped out the door. There were manicured shrubs along the house, so she stepped beyond these on the terrace scanning the area in all directions. The dogs weren't in sight. Maybe they'd get lucky and avoid them altogether this time.

Walking back to the house, she replaced the binoculars in the bag and took out the rope and hook that would get them over the wall again. Securing the pack on her back, she stood, motioned for Sam to follow her. Soundlessly he trailed her out the door, pulled it closed after him. She took no more than a half dozen steps before she stopped abruptly.

Quick reflexes were all that prevented Sam from plowing into her. He grabbed her arms, steadying them both. Juliette looked around carefully, trying to discern what had alerted her. It was another moment before she identified it. There was a faint aroma in the air that hadn't been there even moments earlier when she'd gone out to scout the area.

Cigarette smoke.

Gesturing furiously to Sam, she crouched down, ran silently to a thick stand of bushes and ducked down behind them. Turning her head, she saw that he'd done the same, concealing himself several feet away. Cheek flattened against the decorative rock surrounding the bushes, she waited, barely daring to breathe. The position afforded her little visual. She had to rely on her other senses.

The smell of smoke grew stronger. Juliette strained her ears. There was the crunch of a booted step against stone. Someone was on the terrace they'd vacated only moments before. Adrenaline surged through her veins at the very real possibility of discovery.

Minutes passed in agonizing slowness. Juliette tried to lift her head a fraction, but she couldn't see anything beyond the next bush. It was impossible to tell who was there, near enough that she could stretch her arm from her hiding place and touch the person. Although there was no way to be certain, she didn't think it was Oppenheimer. He smoked, but favored a rare Brazilian brand that smelled faintly of cherries. It was far more likely to be a guard.

The danger of the situation didn't escape her. The bushes weren't especially tall. If the man was looking for something out of the ordinary, she and Sam wouldn't be difficult to spot. And given their positions, they'd be at a distinct disadvantage.

Minutes crawled by. There had been no sign of the dogs yet, but if one of them came around to investigate, it would immediately alert the man to her and Sam's presence. Then things would go very wrong, very, very quickly. And there was nothing Juliette could do right now, but wait.

A burst of static sounded. She was more certain than ever that the person on the terrace was a guard, with a two-way radio clipped to his belt. A word from him and a half dozen men would be swarming the area, making escape all but impossible.

Finally, there was a slight noise. Then a boot moved into her line of vision, grinding a cigarette out against the stone. Moments later footsteps moved across the terrace and away.

Juliette's breath released in a silent rush. Several more minutes were allowed to pass before she raised to a crouch, and peeked over the top of the shrubs. There was no one in sight, but she didn't find that fact reassuring. The guard had appeared only minutes after she'd done a similar scan.

And there was no telling whether any of his companions shared his nicotine habit.

A small rock whizzed by her to land in the bushes. She turned, found Sam staring at her from nearby. He gestured toward the wall and she nodded grimly.

The sooner they made their escape, the sooner she'd breathe easy again.

They rose as one, running across the large expanse of lawn. In the distance she could hear a dog begin to bark. Targeting the same approximate point they'd scaled before, Juliette tossed up the hook. It took two tries to get a secure hold, and then she lost no time scrambling up the attached cable, and over the other side of the wall. She waited for Sam, leaning against the wall, adrenaline pumping so furiously her temples throbbed with it.

As soon as Sam had dropped to the ground beside her, she retrieved the hook and repositioned it, climbing the wall to recover the devices she'd planted on the cameras. Sliding down with the second one, she experienced the familiar euphoria that accompanied every successful job. But coupled with that emotion was the fierce sense of satisfaction that came from duping Oppenheimer under his very nose. She felt like giving a shout of exultation.

She reached for the cable, intent on getting it back in her bag so they could leave. But instead she found herself being swung up in Sam's arms, spun around.

She looked down into his grinning face, minus the mask. "We did it, baby. The whole thing went off without a hitch."

Juliette wasn't certain she totally agreed with his easy assessment, but she didn't utter a protest. Not then, and not when he snatched the hood off her head and covered her mouth with his.

Chapter 10

The night disappeared. The still tangible danger vanished. There were only her lips beneath his, fueling the exhilaration rushing through his veins. With the camera devices still clutched in one hand, she twined her arms around his neck, sent her fingers sliding into his hair.

There was no finesse in the kiss; this wasn't a gradual ease into intimacy. It was raw, unrestrained, filled with all the bottled energy and emotion he'd held in check for the past several hours. Hell. The past several *days*.

His mouth ate at hers, as if the taste of her wasn't already stamped on his brain. As if he would be able to satiate himself with her flavor. He knew even as he tried that he'd fail.

She was as demanding as he was, nipping at his bottom lip and sucking at his tongue. A fireball of heat exploded inside his gut, fueling his hunger. Just kissing her sent a storm of sensation crashing through his system. And all it did was make him need more.

He wanted her naked, hot and twisting beneath him. He wanted to hear her breathless cries while he pleasured her, to hold her while she shattered, and ride the crest buried deep within her. The image was so vivid it took physical effort to tear his mouth from hers, to pull her arms from around his neck and set her away. The acts had him clenching his teeth against the immediate ache of frustration.

He didn't look at her. He couldn't. Not without hauling her back into his arms and finishing this right here, right now. Instead he waited, muscles rigid with tension, until she'd replaced everything in her pack. When she started jogging in the direction of the car, he followed. It didn't help to consider the fact that her pace suggested she needed a physical release, any kind, as badly as he did.

That thought, and the memory of how she felt in his arms, was going to haunt him all the way back to Paris.

"Miles seemed impressed."

Sam glanced over at Juliette. Her head was tipped back against the headrest. Smudges of fatigue shadowed the delicate skin beneath her eyes, which were closed now. She had every right to be exhausted. They both did. There had been very little conversation on the trip home. But the sexual tension had been palpable, making the journey its own kind of hell. After leaving Austria, they'd driven straight to the airport, where'd they'd waited four hours for a flight. His first stop in Paris, of course, had been the safe house where Miles waited.

His mouth twisted. The man had hardly been able to contain his excitement when Sam had given him the high-tech scanner, which was one of the agency's newest gadgets. The information he'd duplicated in Oppenheimer's vault was safely contained in its memory, and all Miles had to do was hook it into his computer to transfer the material to Headquarters at Langley to be decrypted. Juliette was right. He'd all but salivated when he realized what he'd been holding in his hands.

Belatedly, he realized she'd opened her eyes and was looking at him. "He was eager for that information," he said in an understatement. "If it's what we think it is, it's going to be a big help in our... business."

She watched him unblinkingly. "Your business being...an enemy of Oppenheimer."

Although he couldn't identify the inflection in her voice, he nodded. "Rivals, anyway."

"I don't believe you."

Although her blunt statement took him by surprise, he took care not to show it. "He has a lot of interests. You don't believe I might represent someone who the man's crossed over the years?"

"You're very good at that." Her voice was conversational. "Sprinkling just enough truth to your words to make them ring true. Turning questions away by asking other questions."

"It doesn't require all that much talent. We learn it in second-year law school."

"Maybe. But you have a lot of other skills one wouldn't expect to find in a lawyer. Not to mention devices like those little gadgets we used on the cameras back there."

"Which reminds me, you never gave those back."
As an attempt at distraction, he noted, it failed miserably. She was still eyeing him speculatively.

"I've never seen anything like them before. Or
that gadget you used to copy Oppenheimer's files."

He turned his attention to navigating the horrendous Parisian traffic. "You're not the only one with
sources."

"They aren't available, Sam." Her voice was
even. "Those items can't even be gotten on the black
market, and believe me, I would know. I've never
even heard so much as a breath of rumor of their
existence. But if they don't exist, how did you get
them?"

The time for distractions was past. "You should
know that anything is available for a price, Juliette."

She nodded. "I do know it. If the pockets are deep
enough, anything is possible." She paused a beat before going on. "And the U.S. government's pockets
are about as deep as they get."

He didn't even blink at her statement. Beeping the
horn at the slow driver in front of them, he pulled
out to pass him. "What's that got to do with me?"

"I've given it a lot of thought," she said calmly.
Too calmly. "I knew when I met you that you were
more than a lawyer, if you are indeed a lawyer at all.
Too many things just didn't add up. The thoroughness of the investigation you did prior to contacting
me suggests a limitless supply of money. And I doubt
very much you acquired your skills at breaking and
entering at law school. The high-tech gadgets just
helped me put the whole picture together. You're
CIA."

Weaving in and out of the endless stream of cars,

Sam concentrated on not reacting to her words. "You've been watching too much American television. I suppose in your line of work paranoia must become a way of life."

"You're not law enforcement," she went on, as if he hadn't spoken. She had transferred her gaze to the passing city. "No matter how far-reaching the investigation, I would have been offered a deal by now. Probably right away."

"I did offer you a deal," he pointed out.

"Cooperate or be turned over to the authorities." She shrugged, as if it didn't matter. "The police, even the Yard, couldn't ignore laws no matter how important the investigation. There's no use denying it, because I won't believe you."

He looked at her then, a long hard stare. "I admit nothing."

She met his gaze, held it. "What happens with that information, Sam?"

Returning his focus to his driving he said tersely, "It'll be decrypted to determine if it's the data we're looking for."

"And if it's not?"

He hadn't expected the question; hadn't really spent much time considering it. His agent had told him about the file's existence and location shortly before he'd been murdered. From the description he'd received, he didn't doubt that he'd copied the right file. He answered the question anyway, as honestly as he could. "We'd have to reassess. The information exists. It's just a matter of knowing where to find it."

"Over the years I've acquired schematics for the

layout and security of almost every corporate head-quarters he owns.''

Not for the first time, she'd managed to surprise him. ''That had to be expensive.''

''Well there's a delicious sense of irony using money I've gotten from selling his things to finance my endeavors.''

He couldn't help but grin. She sounded so damn smug about it. And she was right. The irony of the deal was beautiful. His grin faded as he considered her earlier words. ''So if you know how to get into any of his holdings…''

''You're welcome to any of the details I've gathered.''

He wasn't going to need her information. He was certain of that. So he didn't know why her response to his next statement seemed so important. ''Let me guess. All that would cost is one of those little camera gadgets you've yet to relinquish.''

Her voice turned reflective. ''Well, if you're offering…''

''I'm not.''

Her shrug was curiously European. ''You're still welcome to it.''

Not, he noted, to her help in acquiring it, just to the security information itself. Still, he could appreciate the generosity of the gesture. Even be touched by it. Juliette Morrow didn't offer anything freely. He'd learned that much about her. Which made her offer doubly precious. It was not, however, the one thing he'd like her to offer. Spontaneously. Without reservations.

Shifting uncomfortably in the seat, he tried to force his mind back to the matter at hand. ''The information I copied has to be verified. Once it has been, you'll be free to go.''

He expected an expression of relief. Or perhaps even a tart response. What he didn't expect was her pensive expression. The emotionless tone. "How much longer?''

"If it checks out, it shouldn't be more than a day or two. Three at the most.''

An empty feeling of loss accompanied the words. Which didn't make sense, given the circumstances. If things checked out it meant they were damn close to nailing Oppenheimer for good. He could get back home for a while until the next assignment. It would be good to see his brothers again, to ride herd on his sister Ana and rib Jones about the wedding plans. But as hard he tried, it wasn't home that filled his mind. It was the woman beside him.

"Three days isn't very long.''

Something in her voice had him looking over at her. And what he saw there almost had him driving into the back of a delivery truck. There was awareness, perhaps a hint of trepidation. But there was also a reflection of the smoldering hunger that had been riding him since they'd met. Seeing it torched his own.

She reached over, her hand hovering for a moment, before settling deliberately, lightly on his thigh. The muscle jumped beneath her palm, and his heart nearly leaped out of his chest before settling down to a slow steady pounding. There was nothing coy about Juliette. When she saw something she wanted, she reached out and took it. That was the very characteristic that had led him to her. The same one that continued to bother him, more than he'd like to admit. But right now, with that wanting turned on him, the trait took on a totally different light.

Her fingers moved upward, hesitated, before sliding down again in a heated stroke that had every nerve ending in his body standing at alert. With his eyes still on the road, he rapidly figured the remaining time before they reached her apartment. Five minutes of driving. Then he still had to park the car. She squeezed his leg lightly and he could feel sweat sheen his upper lip. Another five minutes to get her into the building, up to her penthouse. She traced an imaginary line along his thigh with her fingernail and he accelerated through a yellow light. Horns blared in his wake.

"You're playing a dangerous game." His voice was rough with checked passion.

A tiny smile played across her lips. "I like dangerous games. And you know what, Sam?" She leaned close enough to whisper in his ear. "I think you like them, too. I think you play more than your share of them." Her teeth closed around his earlobe for a quick nibble, before she eased away again. And a fist of desire clenched in his gut even as the truth of her assessment hit him.

Dangerous games. His life was a series of them. Every assignment called for weighing the odds, taking risks. And the time had long since passed when he'd stopped denying it. Duty to his country was only a part of his commitment to the job. The adrenaline highs that came with the missions were as addictive as any drug. Despite his love for his home and family, there was an all too familiar restlessness that would rear up if he spent too long in the law offices or too much time in the States. He needed the rush that came from depending on his wits, with success or disaster hanging in the balance. And he knew Juliette would understand that. Whatever her motivations, she wouldn't have chosen the life she had, wouldn't continue it, if she didn't get that same kind of thrill from the jobs she planned. In that sense, at least, they were all too much alike. The only thing that shook him was the fact she recognized it, too.

Her hand was warm on his leg, and her fingers never stopped moving. Massaging, stroking. He glanced at her. The light in her eyes said she knew exactly what she was doing to him. And it occurred to him in a flash why she was doing it. "You think you'll control this thing between us?" he asked softly. Her eyes widened, as if he'd scored a direct hit. "Think if we let it play out on your terms, in your time, that you'll be able to direct how much you'll give? And take?" His hand went to hers, and he brought it to his lips. "That isn't going to be an option." He closed his teeth around the soft flesh of her palm for an instant, before placing it again on his thigh. This time his hand covered hers. "You play a game with me, you'd better be prepared to risk it all."

Even with his attention divided between the driving and her face, he could see the shock in her expression, the automatic rejection of his words. She was used to guarding her emotions, making her decisions as coolly and as calculatingly as he did. But there wouldn't be cool logic applied to this. He'd make damn sure of it.

"Come over here." His tone made it a dare. With a lift of her brows she accepted, slid nearer so that she was snuggled against his side. For an instant he was reminded of the hours they'd spent in the closet, touching from shoulder to ankle. But then the mission had been between them, something to distract him a little from the flame she ignited every time she got this close. There'd be no diversion this time. And only one conclusion he'd accept.

His blood began to hammer, a hard primal beat. She slid her hand from beneath his and trailed it higher, her index finger tracing the crease between thigh and groin. He jerked in response, swore when the car swerved a bit before he righted it again. Her low laugh told him his earlier words hadn't convinced her. Maybe she'd never met a man who'd demanded…everything. Perhaps her other lovers hadn't cared that she never lowered her guard even when she took them to her bed. But he cared. Enough to dismantle those defenses of hers, if necessary. One by one.

He crooked a finger and ran it lightly along the curve of her breast. His knuckle grazed her nipple. It was turgid, straining against the soft cotton of her top. She didn't quite manage to restrain her sharply indrawn breath. The indication of her response fired his own. Rubbing gently, he circled the nipple with his knuckle, before taking the tip between his thumb and forefinger, squeezing gently.

Her hand clamped on his leg, and a shudder racked her body. He could feel it work its way through her as her body quivered against his. And in that instant he'd have given his considerable inheritance for a soft mattress and a little privacy.

He took the corner to her building too fast, throwing her even closer against him. His hand went to her shirt and he undid the first two buttons with more haste than finesse. Her skin was warm, beckoning a firmer touch, and even as he obeyed the urge, a distant alarm sounded at the back of his mind. Sex was a pleasurable pastime, a way to indulge the senses. He wasn't used to wanting, until it was a fever in the veins, battering him from the inside. Caution should have had him rearing back, rearranging his priorities.

Desperation made caution laughable.

With a screech of brakes he wheeled the car into the parking garage, drove to the top level. The air sizzled with sexual tension, the energy humming and sparking between them. He'd known it'd be like this between them, had sensed it the first time she pressed her mouth against his. But he'd never suspected the way desperation could draw a man tight until the most casual touch threatened to shatter any semblance at civility. She rubbed her free hand over his chest, kneading the muscles beneath, and it took all the strength he could muster to beat back his primitive response.

Throwing the car into park, he turned off the ignition even as he reached for her, pulled her onto his lap with one hard jerk. His mouth found hers, ravenous, devouring. A feral little purr sounded in her throat. The evidence of her desire went to his head faster than his favorite Scotch.

He had just enough control to raise his head, shake it a little to clear the haze of passion. A car was passing by slowly, the driver as intent on watching them as she was on finding a parking spot. It was the reminder he needed that they weren't assured of privacy. Not here. Not yet.

He unlocked the door and shoved it open, tilting the steering wheel up to allow Juliette to slide off his lap. When she did, she pressed her hip snugly against his straining shaft for a moment, and a low groan was torn from him. Poised on the edge of the seat, she looked over her shoulder, and he knew in that instant that the touch hadn't been accidental. Hauling in one deep breath he waited for her to exit the car before following her out. Locking it, he slammed the door shut behind him, slid his arm around her waist, his hand cupping her bottom.

"Wait," she protested breathlessly as he guided her rapidly toward the elevator. "I don't think that's a parking space."

He glanced back at the car, parked at an awkward angle between two yellow lines. "Tough." Reaching the elevator, he jabbed his finger at the button impatiently.

"And our bags are still in the trunk."

The doors slid open, revealing an empty compartment. Sam urged her inside with one firm push on her bottom, and selected the penthouse. When the doors slid shut he slapped his palm over the button that would keep them closed.

"They'll wait." The firestorm she'd ignited in him flared, threatened to erupt as he crowded her against the wall of the elevator and took her lips again. Her mouth was avid, her tongue tangling with his. His free hand went to her shirt and he hooked a finger in it, giving a hard tug. The remaining buttons flew off, bouncing across the area.

His palm skated over her bared stomach, reveling in the feel of warm satiny flesh. She'd feel like that all over, he thought savagely. Like silk just waiting to be stroked. And he was going to touch every inch of her. Find all the secret spots that made her sigh, then moan. Steep himself in her taste and scent until neither of them could tell where one left off and the other began.

His mouth left hers and cruised to her throat, found the pulse there whipping furiously. Oddly enough, the discovery soothed the desperation riding him, just a fraction. Despite her efforts at control, she was having just as hard a time reining in her responses as he was. And that suited him just fine. His hand went to her back, released the hooks on her bra as he scored her throat with his teeth.

"Sam!"

That word held the barest thread of panic even as her head tipped back, allowing him freer access. He skimmed his lips over her jawline, inhaled the perfume she'd dabbed below her ear.

"The elevator could stop...." Her voice trailed off as he stroked his hand on her back, beneath the unfastened bra. He slipped his index finger inside the bottom edge, began inching it toward the front.

"Maybe. But the doors won't open." Her mouth was red, ripe, a little swollen from his. He decided the look suited her. Her breath hitched as his finger moved, one excruciating inch at a time, to her side. She didn't seem to be breathing at all as it traveled at a snail's pace to poise, just beneath her breast.

For a moment all he did was watch her. It was an exquisite torment in its own right. Emotions were chasing over her face, too varied to be identified. Her hands resting lightly on his hips, her lips parted, as if in anticipation of his next move.

This moment had been tantalizing him since the day they met. Since the instant he'd felt her hand in his pocket, her mouth moving expertly on his. Then he'd wanted, badly, to lay her down, to draw exactly this response from her. He'd feared many times that this day would never come. And he'd sometimes feared that it would.

She wouldn't be a woman like any other, to share a lusty coupling and casual parting. He wouldn't be able to dismiss her so easily from his mind, or from his memory. She'd linger there, a tormenting reminder that would take him unaware when he could least afford the distraction. And even knowing it, being certain of it, he couldn't walk away.

He hooked his finger in the bottom of her bra, watched her swallow as it grazed the underside of her breast. Then he drew it upward, baring her to his avid gaze. And any thoughts of future regrets were forgotten.

Her breasts were high, round, the nipples pebbled to hardness. Bending his head, he took one in his mouth and lashed it with his tongue. She pulled him closer, arched her back and he obeyed her unspoken command. His cheeks flexed as he drew strongly from her, taking more of her breast in his mouth, feasting on the taste of her.

She tugged his shirt from his pants, then her hands were skating up his sides. The feel of those soft palms stroking his skin released something savage inside him. This was what he wanted, and yet it wasn't enough. Not nearly enough. She was a fever pounding recklessly through his veins, and every touch ratcheted the temperature up another notch.

Releasing her breast, he admired the sight of her turgid nipple, wet from his suckling, before switching his attention to its twin. Juliette was exploring his chest, kneading the muscles there, tracing a path to his shoulders then back down his sides to start all over again. As she fought to get his shirt off he reluctantly lifted his head and helped her, divesting her of her shirt and bra in one smooth swoop.

Then his mouth found hers. Flesh pressed against flesh, causing a riot of sensation. Control was slipping. Finesse was difficult to summon. Her hands were clutching his biceps, her breasts flattened against his chest. And still he couldn't get enough of her.

The oxygen clogged in his lungs. The air seemed too thick to breathe. There was only the woman in his arms, the responses she was drawing from him. The response he wanted from her in return.

It was several moments before he realized the elevator had stopped. Several more before he could manage to lift his mouth from hers and glance at the floor number. The penthouse.

When the door slid open, he kicked their pile of clothes out first, then, with his hands on Juliette's hips, swung her around and backed her out of the compartment. When her shoulders rested against the wall by her door, he traced her collarbone with his tongue. Unbuttoning her pants, he worked the zipper down to reveal a narrow wedge of black silk.

Leaning forward, Juliette nipped at his shoulder, then assuaged the slight sting with her tongue. The pain only sparked his hunger, honed it to a keener edge. Hands tight on her hips, he battled the visceral demand for release, immediate and primitive. Not now. Not yet. Not until she was crying out from the pleasure he gave her, moaning his name. Not until he'd branded her with his touch, so no other could ever lay a hand on her again without thoughts of him clouding their time together.

The thoughts of any others coming after him had him clenching his jaw to battle back an irrational, primitive fury. A glimmer of it must have been reflected in his expression because when Juliette dragged her eyelids open, she swallowed hard at the sight of him.

"Sam?"

He stroked away the uncertainty in her voice with a soothing hand gliding down her back, pressed a deep wet kiss on her lips to prevent any further questions. They had no future, but the two of them certainly had the present. Now. Here. Today. And he was going to make it last.

Slipping his hands into her unfastened pants, he pushed them down over the provocative curve of her hips. Along the silky expanse of thigh, until he was kneeling before her, divesting her of all her clothing except the scrap of panties.

His chest tightening, he stared up at her, imprinting the picture she made on his memory. Her earlier uncertainty had faded, and the only emotion that showed on her face was desire. Her tangle of dark hair covered her bare shoulders, teased the tops of her breasts. Her skin was the color of rich cream, inviting a caress. With her curves promising the sweetest ride into heaven, she personified sin, wickedly seductive.

As if reading his thoughts, her lips tilted. With a deliberate stretch of her leg, she trailed her foot lightly up the inside of his thigh, to circle suggestively around the bulge in his pants.

"One of us is overdressed."

Taking her small foot in his hands, he massaged the arch with his thumbs before setting it on the floor and rising. "Not from where I'm standing." He cupped her face in his hands and kissed her, deep and rawly carnal, holding nothing back, demanding the same response in return. He got that, and more. Juliette wrapped her arms around his neck, fingers threading through his hair. His mouth ate at hers, as if to assuage the heavy ache that had settled in his loins.

She gave a little gasp of surprise when his arms cupped her bottom, lifted her off the floor. Her legs wrapped around his waist instinctively, and he pressed her back against the wall, dipping his head to take one nipple in his mouth. He sucked from her until she was twisting against him, the notch of her thighs rubbing against his manhood. He thrust against her, one heavy surge of his hips, and a moan was ripped from her throat.

A wholly masculine surge of satisfaction filled him. The sound of her passion stripped away the last veneer of civility he possessed. There would be nothing between them but this. The pleasure they gave each other as they rode the vicious ache of desire to its inevitable shattering conclusion. Just the thought of it, the wild release that was just tantalizingly out of reach, made his blood rage.

He lifted his head enough to rasp out, "Open the door."

Juliette was slow to respond. Movements sluggish, she reached out, hand trembling on the keypad. After a couple failed attempts she recited the combination for him and he punched it in with barely restrained force. With her still wrapped around him, he strode into the apartment and to her bedroom.

The sun was still bright as it streamed into the room, patterning the bed with ribbons of light. He laid her back on the bed, obeying her unspoken command as she pulled him down with her. Kicking off his shoes, he skimmed his mouth over her shoulders, down her arms and began a slow, thorough exploration of her body.

He found soft secret places that were exquisitely sensitive. Places that made her sigh, others that made her moan. The bend of an elbow. The crease behind her knees. He was on a journey of discovery, taking as much pleasure in the task as he gave.

A whimper of frustration escaped her and she clutched at his shoulders, tried to pull him back up to her. "Now."

With slitted eyes he studied her, brushing her heavy mass of hair back from face. "Not yet." He nuzzled the baby soft skin in back of her ear, his hand stroking her stomach not quite soothingly. His fingers grazed the silk covering her mound, found it damp. "There's more. Give me more." He covered her mouth with his even as he moved aside the elastic band of her panties, found the wet heat beneath. Her body shuddered and bucked beneath him as he parted her slick folds, penetrated her with one smooth stroke of his finger.

Her heels pressed against the bed, her back arched. She was moist hot silk as he stroked her, her nails biting into his shoulders as she slowly went wild beneath him. And need slashed through him like a flash of a blade, edgy and keen.

Sam levered himself up enough to strip the panties from her before divesting himself of the rest of his clothes. He was searching through his pants pockets when she reached over, opened the drawer on the nightstand to reveal some foil packets. As he unwrapped one she swayed forward, delicately licked a pearly drop of liquid from the tip of his manhood. His hips jerked in involuntary reaction, one hand spearing through her hair to cup her head. It took every ounce of control he possessed to allow her to unroll the latex over his length, with excruciating slowness. When she'd accomplished that task she cupped him, exploring him with those slender, clever fingers.

He withstood the exquisite torture as long as he could. But a red mist was hazing his vision, signaling the end to his control. He reached for her, hands rougher than he meant them to be when he tossed her back on the bed. Nudging her knees apart he settled between her legs, fit himself intimately to the notch in her thighs. Her slumberous eyes were dark depths of desire that an unwise man could drown in. Her swath of hair was a pool of black silk across the bedspread. And in that instant Sam knew he'd never wanted a woman like this before, until his mind reeled with the strength of the longing. With a flicker of desolation he wondered if he ever would again.

Her hips surged under his, impatient and demanding. He rubbed his lips over hers, even as he reached for her knee, pressed it toward her thigh. He used

the position to ease his penetration, sliding inside her
with one hard thrust.

Juliette bucked beneath him, body shuddering,
arms clasped tightly around his back. He couldn't
breathe. Couldn't think. She was tight as a fist around
him, and he could feel the delicate pulsations as her
inner muscles adjusted to his entry. Each of her
movements seated him more deeply inside her, and
his world narrowed in a whirling vortex until she was
the focus. She was all he could see. All he could
feel.

He surged against her in a slow steady rhythm,
ignoring the bite of her nails as she urged him
deeper. Faster. But when her legs climbed his hips,
clasped around his waist, he knew there was no denying the inevitable. They moved together in a
greedy race of urgency. He watched her eyes go
blind as she crested, swallowed her cry. And when
her body went taut beneath him, drawn tight with
shock and pleasure, he hammered himself into her,
waiting for her limbs to go lax with the shuddering
release. Only then did he allow himself to dive into
that freefall of pleasure. And as he followed her over
his own jagged brink, all he heard was his name on
her lips.

The sunlight had long since faded. Sam and Juliette dozed, woke to reach for each other again, then
drifted into light slumber before the desire started
anew. She was sprawled on top of him now, her body
lax and boneless after their last bout of lovemaking.
He stroked her lightly, feeling the delicate vertebra,

the rounded curves of her bottom. But his mind wasn't on the satiny texture of her skin. Something far heavier weighed on it.

"I could arrange for you and your grandmother to go to another country," he said more abruptly than he'd intended. He felt her body grow still, and cursed his clumsiness. He was capable of far more finesse, but for some reason this issue seemed beyond diplomacy. "Anywhere you want. Any identity you want. I doubt you lack for money, but if you do, I can get you some. Enough to set you up in a shop. Pay for college. Whatever you choose."

Her voice, when it came, was carefully expressionless. "I can already go anywhere I want. *Be* anyone I want."

She couldn't have said more clearly that she didn't need him. Not his help. And certainly not his concern for her. "It's only a matter of time until you're caught," he said quietly. His eyes were sightless as he stared into the darkness. "If not by law enforcement then by someone Oppenheimer has hired. Either you end up in prison or dead. What kind of choice is that?"

When she would have moved away from him his arms tightened, keeping her in place. "It's my choice." The words were soft, but with a note of finality. "I…can't explain. But I know what I'm doing, and I…have to finish it. You wouldn't understand. But the risks I take are worth the end result."

Rolling her to her back, he urged, "Think about it. Do you really want to take the chance your grandmother will end up alone? Or even go to prison with you?'' The mutinous expression that came across her face made him want to shake her. ''For God's sake, wake up before it's too late. No amount of money is worth the danger you put yourself in. Give it up. Before it's too late.''

He was prepared for a rousing argument. A heated discussion in which he could make her see reason with flawless logic. But he wasn't prepared for her face to soften with an emotion he couldn't quite discern. Her hand rose to cup his jaw and her words, when they came, were spoken in an aching whisper. ''I can't.''

He rolled away from her, filled with a dismal certainty. No amount of arguing was going to persuade her. Her refusal to listen could only have one result. He almost choked on an unfamiliar surge of helplessness. Because he was equally sure the path she'd chosen was going to lead to her eventual destruction.

It was that certainty that had him pushing further. ''Why?'' Frustration edged his tone. ''What's so damn important about this vendetta you have against Oppenheimer that you won't...''

Somewhere in the apartment a phone rang, interrupting him. He sat up, identifying the sound as a cell phone. His first impression was that it was awfully early for Miles to have word back on that file.

But by the second ring he realized his mistake. Getting out of bed, he switched on the lamp sitting on the bedside table and strode naked to his luggage. It wasn't the phone he used to communicate with Miles. It was his private cell. The one whose number was known only to his family. He answered, fully expecting to hear Jones on the other end. The last person he expected to hear from was his oldest brother, James.

The conversation was brief, chillingly succinct. Long after it had ended, Sam found himself clutching the phone, tamping down wave after wave of urgent, violent emotion.

"Sam? Is something wrong?"

He felt Juliette's hand on his shoulder. It seemed to take a great deal of effort to turn toward her. Even more to formulate a response. "It's my younger brother," he said grimly. "He's been shot."

Chapter 11

Juliette had always found her apartment to be more than roomy. But after watching Sam pace it for four hours, the space seemed to have shrunk to the size of a handkerchief. For the hundredth time he went to the window, lifted the blinds to peer out, then dropped them again. She doubted he really saw anything when he looked out. And her heart, that organ she'd carefully shielded for most of her life, ached for him.

She didn't have siblings to worry about. There was only her grandmother, and to a lesser degree Jacques, who were close enough to elicit this kind of emotion from her. But she imagined she knew how she'd feel if one of them were lying on a surgeon's table a continent away. Helpless. And because that emotion would burn, there'd be fury as well, that she couldn't be there. Couldn't change things through sheer force of will. It was doubtful that Sam felt much differently.

"You could get a flight out," she suggested. She'd heard him on the phone with someone called Jones, heard him tell the person to do that very thing. But not once had Sam mentioned doing the same, despite the worry that seemed to be eating him alive. "Airlines make special arrangements for family emergencies."

He was shaking his head before she'd even finished her statement. "I can't leave. Not with this thing breaking on Oppenheimer."

Not for the first time, she wondered just what 'thing' he thought he had on the man, but now wasn't the time to ask. Her attention had shifted to his leg. She didn't think it was her imagination that over the course of the past few hours, he'd taken to rubbing his thigh more and more frequently. No doubt it had stiffened up on him. The only surprise was that it hadn't given him problems before this. Their exertions on the estate had been more than a little physically taxing, and the car and plane rides couldn't have helped.

"Maybe you should take your weight off your leg for a while."

He gave an impatient roll of his shoulder, and continued to prowl the room. "It's fine."

"If it were fine, I doubt very much you'd be massaging it," she pointed out.

"I'm not..." He looked down, seemed to be surprised that he was doing just that. He let his hand drop to his side. But he didn't stop pacing the area, a sleek dangerous jungle cat on the prowl.

She wasn't a woman used to offering comfort.

Even the temptation to do so was foreign. She didn't get close enough to people to allow them to matter. Most people were satisfied with a shallow civil veneer, she'd found. Few had seemed to look for more. And only Sam had been compelled to dig further, to strip layers away from the surface until he'd discovered…far more about her than was comfortable.

The reminder had her looking away. He'd gotten closer to her last night than any other man had ever been permitted. Not that there had been a conscious decision on her part to allow it. She was an expert at remaining detached, under any circumstances. But he'd made that impossible. Heat suffused her at the memory. There had been only hunger and emotion, a flashing firestorm of the senses. And that meant he was far more of a danger to her than any other man she'd ever known. Because emotion shifted priorities. Affected decision-making. And her decisions had been made long, long ago.

So it shouldn't have mattered so much to realize that she'd disappointed him last night with her answer. Pressing her lips together, she told herself it didn't matter. He couldn't know what he was asking her to give up. What he was asking her to forgive. She knew he was an honorable man. And perhaps one with his sense of decency would have found a way to live with what had happened. But she'd only found one way. And she couldn't turn away from it now.

Sam dropped into an easy chair across from her. Reaching over, he picked up her favorite ivory piece and worried it with his fingers.

It occurred to her that their roles had switched, at least for the moment. She was the one who thought best on the move, while he'd always remained still. Not necessarily peaceful, not with that lethal energy that always radiated from him, but giving a semblance, at least, of calm.

She'd never know why she did it. But she rose, went to the kitchen and poured him a tumbler of the Scotch he'd ordered the first night he'd so infuriated her by insisting on staying in her apartment. Going to him, she placed it in his hand and said, "Come on."

He glanced at the glass, and then at her. "Where are we going?" Standing, he set the ivory piece on the table and obediently trailed after her to the master bath. Then watched, with a bemused expression as she turned the jets on in the hot tub. "I didn't expect another invitation into here."

"Actually, it's your *first* invitation here, since last time you really didn't wait to be invited."

He didn't smile, but his face softened a little, as if the memory pleased him. "A polite hostess wouldn't have mentioned that."

The water was bubbling and frothing. Stepping away from the tub, she looked at him. "Unfortunately for you, I'm neither polite, nor your hostess. Which is why I'd rather have you soak that leg than wait for you to collapse entirely. I wouldn't make a very good nurse."

Looking torn, he said, "I need to wait to hear from James."

With brisk movements she was taking out towels, setting them near the tub. "The last I checked, cell phones were perfectly functional in bathrooms. You can take the call in here if you can manage not to drop the phone in the tub."

Because her attention was on her task, she was surprised to find her hand taken in his. Even more surprised when he lifted it to his lips, dropped a kiss on her palm. Her pulse fluttered.

"I'll agree on one condition. That you join me." She must have looked as stunned as she felt because he went on to add, "We established that first night, there's plenty of room for two in that tub."

Everything inside her violently rejected the suggestion. What she needed right now was distance. Time to regroup. No doubt it was a momentary lapse caused by exhaustion and proximity, but he'd gotten too close, too fast. And so she stalled. "Someone should stay out there." She waved a hand vaguely toward the door. "Miles might call. With word on the file."

"The last I checked, cell phones were perfectly functional in bathrooms." He managed to repeat her words with a perfectly sober expression as he passed by her. "I'll go get it."

Drawing in a decidedly shaky breath, Juliette straightened her shoulders. She could deal with this, she thought firmly. Handling things was her area of expertise. And handling men had never posed any particular problem in the past. Sam was no different, because she wouldn't *allow* him to be. He'd be gone in a day or two. If she felt a pang at the thought she was determined not to acknowledge it. And once he was gone, she'd go on with her life.

She believed that implicitly because she needed to. And when Sam reentered the bathroom, second cell phone in hand, the look of surprise on his face to find her stripped and in the tub was almost worth the knots in her stomach. Almost.

He made it easy, she thought minutes later, so incredibly easy to relax with him and pretend, at least for a time, that things were not nearly as complicated as they seemed. The groan of satisfaction he'd given when he'd stepped into the water made her certain that her decision here had been the correct one. And even when he positioned himself between her legs, his back resting against her breasts, his head pressed against her shoulder, she had no doubt she could keep a part of herself separate. Her defenses were too well developed to fail her again.

He was silent for a while, but she could feel the tension seep from his limbs, one fraction at a time. She took a loofah sponge from the side of the tub, dipped it in the water, then squeezed it over his chest. The repetition of her motions soothed them both.

"I remember one other time Cade was in the hospital, I was just this worried. Terrified, really."

Her hand stilled on his torso. "He's been shot before?"

"No. He'd fallen off the garage roof. Broke his collarbone and his right ankle. Honesty compels me to admit that I might have given him a small shove. Accidentally, of course."

She tugged at the hair on his chest. "Beast. Please tell me you were a kid."

"I was ten, and he was eight. We'd made our own hang gliders, wanted to try them out. Seeing as he was smaller, lighter, seemed only logical that he go first."

"Perfectly logical."

A smile sounded in his voice, as if the memory was a good one. "Once I figured he was going to live, I started giving thought to my more immediate demise. Had my grandmother found out what we'd been doing, I'd have been in the bed next to him.''

It wasn't the first time he'd mentioned his grandmother. She was curious despite herself. ''Your grandmother lived with you?''

He slid his hand up her wet thigh, a not quite innocent glide. ''From the time I was nine. My parents had been killed in an accident and there was no one else.''

There was no one else. The words resonated, more deeply than they should have. She knew what it was like to be alone, although certainly not at the age he and his siblings had been.

Reaching for his drink, he tipped the glass to his lips then continued his story. ''I was pretty grateful Cade lived, of course. Even more so when he kept quiet about what had happened. That was before I realized that he was going to make me pay for my part in it. Had to wait on him hand and foot all summer long. Always thought he stayed on crutches an extra month, just so I'd have to fetch and carry for him.''

''Served you right,'' she said unsympathetically.

He set the glass back on the edge of the tub. ''Guess I knew that, even back then, so I didn't complain too much.'' She could feel the tension start creeping back into his limbs. ''Dammit all to hell, why doesn't that phone ring?''

She resumed trickling water over his chest. ''Is he in the same line of work as you?''

''He's a police detective.'' With a neat verbal sidestep he managed to skirt addressing part of her question. ''One of the youngest to make grade in his department. We were all so damn proud. With his talent for investigation, I always knew he'd be a cop or a criminal. He had a talent for blackmail when we were kids. Don't remember how many times I had to pay him off to keep quiet about one of my misdeeds.''

There was something about the cadence of his speech, she thought, that reminded her of the deep south. ''Why do I have the feeling that you kept him pretty solvent throughout childhood?''

He tipped his head back and pressed a kiss to her chin. ''It's that suspicious mind of yours. I don't know where you got such a low opinion of me. I've been a perfect gentleman.'' His statement might not have been so outrageous if he hadn't been stroking her upper thigh, his fingers grazing her intimately.

Pushing his hand away, she observed, ''Perfection is so often in the eye of the beholder.'' The pinch her words elicited was almost worth it. ''And I won't even comment on the gentleman...'' Her words trailed off as a phone rang, her gaze going from one phone to the other. Sam reacted more quickly, straightening in the tub so suddenly that the water splashed over the edge. Swiping his hand on a towel, he grabbed one of the phones and answered it tersely.

It was a moment before she recognized the phone that he'd answered was his personal one. And when his body sagged, leeching his muscles of strength, she found herself hoping, more than was comfortable, that it was relief causing it. His next words confirmed it.

''But he's going to be okay?'' He listened, then chuckled, a sound she'd never heard from him before. ''Yeah, that sounds like him. I'm not worried about it. Stick Ana by his bedside and let him try to get by her.''

She was prepared for the wide grin on his face when he set the phone down, but not for the bone-crushing hug he caught her in immediately afterward. "I'm glad your brother is all right," she managed, despite her strangled lungs.

"He's a tough one. Dug three bullets out of his chest and he's already bitching about getting back to work. Guess since I'm not there to wait on him he figures there's no point in staying in bed."

There was, she was almost certain, a compliment to the man somewhere in there. "Sounds a lot like his brother. How long did the wound in your leg keep you down?"

He shrugged off her question. "Mine was from a knife, not a bullet." Leaning down, he nipped at her neck. "The doctor did recommend regular sexual activity as therapy." They were kneeling in the tub, facing each other, and his hands were sliding over her hips. Lower.

"That's uh…interesting advice," she gasped, as his fingers encroached on a very sensitive area. "I doubt it's made it to the medical journals."

He cupped his hands in the water and dribbled it down her chest. "That's where you come in." His words held a laugh, although his expression was sober enough. "You could help me with the research." His fingers slicked over her breasts, circling the nipples, before pausing to roll them between his thumbs and forefingers. "Purely in the interest of medicine, of course."

There was a huge knot in her throat, making it impossible to swallow. "Of course." The tiny drops of water clinging to his collarbone were a temptation she couldn't resist. Leaning forward, she licked them off. This lighthearted approach to sex was unfamiliar to her, as unfamiliar as the sudden rush of pleasure that threatened to swamp her system.

"Never let it be said—" she scraped her fingernail lightly across his nipple, watched him react "—that I refused to do my part for science."

A tiny alarm sounded in her mind, where reason was rapidly receding, reminding her of the vow she'd made earlier. It was easily quieted. This wasn't so dangerous. Not really. Languidly, she smoothed her hands over his chest, tracing bone and sinew with fingertips moments before she followed with her lips. Surely a moment out of time wasn't so much to ask when moments were all they had to offer one another.

She dodged the dart of pain that accompanied the thought and focused on the sensations careening inside her. He had quick, clever hands, and had already learned the places on her body that made her weak, turned her boneless. She caught her breath when he took the lobe of her ear between his teeth, then turned her head, nipped at his jaw. Her hands slipped lower in the water and found him, hard and ready. When her fingers closed around his length, his hips jerked, and she gave a slow smile. It wasn't quite fair that all he had to do was slick his tongue down her throat to shoot her pulse to riot. Evidence of his response somehow balanced the scales. She tilted her head to give him better access and slid her fingers along his hardness, up and down in a slippery dance that had his jaw clenching, his muscles tensing.

His arm banded around her back, quick and sneaky, while his mouth crushed down on her. It was hot, greedy, with enough bite to send the blood siz-

zling under her skin. She rubbed against him, enjoying the delicious friction of wet flesh sliding against
wet flesh. She could taste his desperation as his lips
twisted against hers, a wild primitive flavor that
made the blood chug through her veins.

This exultant passion was new, unexpected. Sensation slapped against sensation as they pressed together, fighting to get closer. Then his hand swept
down her thigh, between her legs, and he gave her
more. With her mouth still captured beneath his he
plunged his fingers into her, swallowing the cry that
sprang from her lips as he drove her up. Then higher.

Her climax ripped through her, a violent shock to
the system that left her shattered and weak. It should
have been fulfilling, would have been, had he not
kept driving, pushing her further.

Satisfaction melded into renewed hunger. She
wanted, as she'd never wanted before. Needed him
where she was still throbbing, wet and aching. Her
fingers slid down, found the heavy sac below his
manhood and explored him, felt him tighten at her
touch.

Then he was pulling her to her feet, water splash-
ing precariously over the edge of the tub. With one
hand he reached behind him, searched blindly, and
she leaned toward him, scraped her teeth over his flat
nipple. The planes of his chest begged to be caressed.
His narrow hips and hard masculine buns invited exploration.

But he was past the point of teasing. He sat on the
edge of the seat in the tub, pulled her between his
legs with hands that stopped just short of rough. She
balanced her hands on his wide shoulders, taking a
moment to savor the picture he made, to store it away

in her memory. Skin slicked with moisture, narrow poet's face etched with desire. Then she straddled him, taking him inside her an inch at a time.

He felt thick, huge. His earlier ministrations had left her delicate inner tissues swollen, and she rocked gently on his lap, each movement taking him a little deeper. When she was fully impaled by that hard length she remained motionless for a moment, searching for a semblance of control that seemed far out of reach.

But in the next instant he clutched her hips, drove himself upward in an action that sent thoughts of restraint spinning away. There was only the rhythmic pumping of his hips, each motion burying him inside her more completely. There was a moment's panic, at having her senses, her body invaded so totally. She managed to drag her eyelids open, focus on him. His head was thrown back, his teeth bared as if in the throes of exquisite agony. She captured his bottom lip in her teeth ungently, and his hand slipped between their bodies. As he fondled her, the heel of his palm pressed against her lower belly in a constant steady pressure that had her writhing against him, demanding, and receiving more.

And this time when the pleasure swept her up and over that jagged edge, she took him with her.

Juliette took her time dressing, fixing her hair. It gave her a chance to steady nerves that were still skipping and pulsing. Just thinking about those long moments lying collapsed and spent against Sam, feeling the shudders wrack his body, was enough to send a new skitter through her system. She needed time…to wedge a safe distance between them again.

It hadn't occurred to her until later that he must have brought a condom in with him when he'd retrieved the other phone. The sheer sexual confidence imbued in the action would have annoyed if it hadn't proved justified. She ought to be glad he'd thought of it. It was doubtful either of them were thinking clearly enough to have made it to the bedroom. She was used to taking physical risks, but had always been careful to avoid such intensely personal ones.

She looked in the mirror, examining her flawless makeup critically. Clothes and makeup could be an effective tool for shoring up defenses. She preferred not to dwell on the reason she felt the need for both.

Sam was on the couch wearing only a pair of jeans and an unbuttoned shirt. His bare feet were propped on a century-old marble-topped table, a fresh glass of Scotch on the matching table beside him.

She gave his feet a pointed look, one that faded when she saw the expression on his face. His countenance was contemplative, and there was a look in his eye, a glint of resolve that filled her with a sense of foreboding.

An innate feminine instinct had her skirting the couch and seating herself in the armchair across from him. She took more time than necessary crossing her legs, smoothing her dress, before coolly meeting his gaze with her own. "You look deep in thought."

He nodded, reached for his glass and took a drink. "As a matter of fact, I was thinking of you."

Her pulse jittered oddly, but she merely skimmed her brows upward. "Really."

"I was wondering what you were going to do. When this is over."

She didn't answer for a moment. Couldn't. It

wasn't as if she hadn't been longing for that time, when she could go forward with her life without his interference. But the thought of returning to her time line brought her no satisfaction right now. And she blamed the man sitting before her for that. "I had plans long before I met you. They still need to be implemented."

"You mean you'll keep targeting Oppenheimer."

Something in that cold flat tone of his made her eye him carefully. Whatever he'd been thinking about while he sat out here alone hadn't pleased him. "I don't think either of us are in a position to be completely open with each other, are we?"

"On the contrary, I'm willing to share some information with you that you'll find interesting." He rattled the ice in his glass. "You haven't said much, but I'm assuming there's something personal at stake between you and our mutual quarry." His remark lodged with unerring accuracy somewhere in the vicinity of her chest. It was suddenly difficult to breathe. "So I'm wondering what you're going to do when he's no longer available."

It would have been far easier to look away. She refused to even blink. She'd considered the possibility, of course, especially once she'd reached the conclusion about who Sam was working for. Her time line was going to have to be sped up. It wasn't strict adherence to the schedule that mattered most, at any rate. It was the end result that counted. Her words didn't lack confidence when she said, "My plans are flexible."

He leaned forward then, speared her with a look. "You're going to continue to target him while he's in prison? Or in a coffin? Because that's where he's going, you know. One way or the other, he's going down. And it won't be long now. Miles called a few minutes ago. Headquarters has decoded the information in the file, and it's the evidence we've been looking for.''

Her chest abruptly hollowed out. It hadn't been three days at all. Their time together was over. She took a fortifying breath. Well, she'd known this time was coming. And it was probably best that they separate now. Cleaner. Things had taken on a sense of urgency once she learned that the CIA was targeting Oppenheimer, as well. The knowledge called for a change in strategy, a fast-forward speed to reach her goal.

Sam was still speaking, in that flat expressionless voice she was quickly coming to detest. ''He should be in custody by tomorrow. So I'm asking you, once he's out of the way, will your risk-taking be over, or are you merely going to move on to another patsy?''

His words seemed to come from a distance. Everything inside her violently rejected his first statement. ''No…you said you were investigating him.'' She almost trembled with the effort it took to remain still. To keep her voice steady. ''It will take time to put everything together. Weeks, at least.''

The slow shake of his head negated her words, and sent panic sprinting up her spine. ''We've long suspected that he's been selling arms to terrorist groups all over the world. All we needed was proof. The file gave us that. He's been smuggling the arms by water. The file contained dates of shipments and the names of his customers.'' He gave a humorless smile. ''We would have had a witness, but he wound up dead.

People who cross Oppenheimer tend to end up that way.''

If there was a warning in his words, it was wasted on her. She knew too well what the man was capable of. Had waited too long to make him pay for just one of his many crimes. She wasn't going to allow that opportunity to be snatched away. Not now. Not when she was so close.

Surging to her feet, she circled the chair, clutched the back of it tightly. ''I just need a little more time. Then you can do what you want with him.'' A note had entered her voice that came uncomfortably close to pleading. Hearing it, hating it, she hardened her tone. ''He's guilty of a great many things, Sam. And I'm going to be the one to make him pay for one of them.''

''Why you?'' There was genuine concern threading his words. She knew, if she looked at his face, she'd see it reflected there, as well. ''What in God's name did he do to you?''

Slowly she lifted her gaze from her white-knuckled grip on the chair to meet his eyes. ''He murdered my mother.''

Chapter 12

It was amazing, Juliette thought, how quickly icy calm had followed her earlier panic. The emotion was infinitely preferable to the pain that could rear from the memory, ripping at her heart with great fanged jaws.

But it was still harder than it should have been to continue to meet Sam's gaze, to see the inevitable questions in his eyes. She'd never felt the need to provide the answers to anyone before. But if he was right, all her plans, years in the making, were at risk. There'd be no satisfaction in having Oppenheimer in prison or dead before she'd completed what she'd set out to do. First he had to lose *everything*. Bitterness curled through her stomach. It was only just. He'd robbed her of that. He'd stolen her childhood, slicing away that time of innocence and showing her what it was to live in constant fear. He'd destroyed her family. Killed her mother.

Her fingers curled into fists. Sam could do what he wanted to the man, but only after she'd destroyed him, and let him know just who had been stealing everything he most prized over the years. It was little enough to ask, she thought. And she wouldn't be denied it.

First, though, the man before her would have to be convinced. Time had just become a priceless commodity. And Sam Tremaine could grant her that time. If she could just make him understand what was at stake.

Her voice when it came sounded rusty. "You guessed once that I was from America. I was certain there were no traces of the U.S. in my accent."

"There aren't, usually. Your French accent is flawless. There's just a certain flatness to the vowels when you're under stress." He stopped when she glared at him, and shrugged. "I'm trained to notice things like that."

It was ridiculous to allow that to smart, so she ignored the reaction. "My grandmother was from a well-to-do French family, although they lost much of their wealth in the war. She married an American soldier and after the war they went to America, settled down. My mother was born in Pittsburgh, and that's where I grew up, too."

It was difficult to keep the emotion from creeping into her voice, into her heart. Firmly, she banished it. The only feeling that had served her for the past decade was the thirst for revenge. There was no room in her life for more.

She managed a brisk tone as she went on. "I never knew my father. He died when I was three. We lived with my grandmother as long as I can remember. My grandfather had died before I was born. The summer I was nine my grandmother took us to France to show us her homeland. We visited what was left of her family's properties. But it was in Paris that my mother met Hans Oppenheimer.''

For just a moment she wished for the drink still sitting within Sam's reach. ''My grandmother didn't approve of him. And when she saw how quickly my mother fell for him, her disapproval grew. She did everything she could to keep them apart.'' Juliette still remembered the arguments, a new frightening development in her young life. Her mother and grandmother had never disagreed about anything before that she could remember. But Oppenheimer had changed everything. ''When grandmother went back to America, my mother and I stayed.''

The recollection of those early days seemed almost surreal. Things had changed quickly, violently, later, but she could still remember how happy her mother had been at first. How full of joy and fun. She'd believed in fairy tales and happily-ever-afters. For a while, Juliette had, too.

''We started traveling with him, and it wasn't long before we all lived together.'' And that, she thought, as nerves knotted in her stomach, was when things began to alter. ''He grew jealous and demanding. Then he became abusive. He's a man who enjoys possessing things. We were his possessions, at least she was. And I was a tool to keep her in line.''

''She could have left,'' he murmured, not unsympathetically. ''That was no place for an impressionable kid.''

Although he was wrong, it meant more than it should have that his first concern was for her, for the child she'd been. "She tried to, three times that I remember. The farthest we ever got was to the street. He had people everywhere, and we'd be brought back. Then I wouldn't see her for days after. But I'd hear her. Hear what he did to her behind locked doors."

Her palms had gone damp in the retelling. She rubbed them on the fabric of the chair she was still clutching. "We were in a strange country, with no money and no friends. Neither of us spoke the language. My grandmother grew alarmed when she didn't hear from us and came back to France to see us. She was beginning to make trouble for Oppenheimer, so he had her put away. The sanitarium he selected was secure and it was discreet." And if keeping a sane woman drugged and tied to her bed had bothered the owner's conscience, that small upset had been soothed by the large monthly payments he received in return.

With her index finger, she traced the pattern on the material. "Now he had all three of us under his power, and we were each used to control the others. Displeasing him meant that one of the three would be punished." Her lips stretched in a humorless smile. "He was big on punishment."

"Did he hurt you?"

It wasn't his words that struck her, but the lethal tone with which he uttered them. She blinked, shook off the haze of memory. There was menace in his expression and it took a moment to realize it was on her behalf. And another moment for a ribbon of warmth to unfurl within her, melting a bit of the ice that had lodged there. "My mother demeaned herself regularly to keep that from happening." And she'd accepted that, without ever managing to shake off the accompanying guilt.

"They went out one night, I'm not sure where. He enjoyed showing her off in public. He must have made an excuse, pretended to come back looking for something…" Not by so much as a quiver did her voice betray the revulsion that snaked down her spine at the memory. "Luckily, my mother didn't trust him. She followed him back to the building and came in just in time to keep him from raping me." In time to see the bruises on her face, and the torn clothing. In time to find him on top of her, shoving her legs apart and loosening his pants….

"She knocked him off me and then he went after her. When she screamed at me to run, I did." Even shocked, frightened out of her mind, she knew she'd never make it past his people at the doors. So she'd gone to the balcony, climbed up to the roof and jumped. Fueled by fear and a deep-seated rage, she'd kept leaping from one rooftop to the other. When she'd gone down to the street she'd been several buildings away and taken her chance to run. "I never saw my mother again. I was fourteen."

"Where'd you go? What did you do?"

She let out a breath she didn't realize she'd been holding. "First I went to the sanitarium where my grandmother was being held. With a little imagination, it was astonishingly easy to whisk her out of there one night. It took several days for the medication to wear off, so she was thinking clearly. We stayed in homeless shelters for a while. Then we started to plan a way to get my mother away from him."

Restless, she was driven to move, to pace the same

area he'd prowled earlier that day. "We knew we couldn't depend on the police. He was a powerful man, even back then, and what kind of credibility would a teenager and a woman declared incompetent have? It was a shock to discover that we had no resources to speak of. He must have forged her name, because somehow he'd managed to sell my grandmother's home in America, and liquidate her assets. So we were homeless, penniless and on the run. He had men looking for us, and we weren't necessarily to be delivered to him alive. So we went into hiding.

"Grandmother had been active during the war in the French Resistance. She contacted a man she'd known then. He'd expanded a bit on the skills he'd acquired stealing information from the Germans." The thought of Jacques brought a bit of warmth seeping into her heart. "He bribed one of the servants and found that my mother hadn't been seen since the day after I left."

"And you suspected Oppenheimer had killed her."

"I know he did," she said flatly. She'd hung on to hope far longer than was reasonable, but there had come a time when she'd been forced to accept the inevitable. She'd carry the grief for her lifetime. "My mother and I had talked about escape often enough. We'd planned where to meet if we got split up. We had someone covering that spot for more than a year after she disappeared. She never came, which meant she *couldn't* come."

"And you began to plot your revenge," he said quietly.

"We stayed with Grandmother's friend until we could afford another place. He arranged for our new identities and became my mentor. I was sixteen when I pulled my first job alone.'' The memory of lifting that small but priceless Dali from a museum in Brussels still gave her a glow, dissipating some of the sorrow. She turned on her heel, paced across the room again. "The money from its sale bought us a home. And the money from the next theft bought us the specs and blueprints of one of Oppenheimer's corporations.''

"Juliette.'' He caught her hand when she would have passed by him and held it until she met his gaze. The sympathy she saw there had a hard ball knotting in her throat. "God knows, you have reason to hate him, probably more than most. But you've made him pay, over and over through the years. Let it be enough.''

"It's not enough!'' She snatched her hand from him and curled the fingers tightly enough to have the nails biting into her palm. "It won't be enough until he's lost everything that means something to him. Until he knows what it's like to have nothing…no home, no reputation, no loved ones. And then I'll come forward and make sure he realizes who took all those things from him. And why.'' The speech had her shaking with determination. That vow had kept her sane for a decade. And she wasn't going to let anyone stand in the way of seeing it through. Not even Sam Tremaine.

"That's what you're planning? To confront him and rub his face in what you've done?'' Disbelief was in his voice, along with something that sounded suspiciously like fear. She dismissed the thought as soon as it occurred. She'd never seen Sam display fear, or any emotion remotely close to it. It was ridiculous to think he'd feel it on her behalf.

"I like to think I'll have a bit more finesse than that, but yes, in the end I will confront him. That's why I need a little more time." This was the most important part of the conversation, the reason she'd stripped her soul bare for him in a way she'd done for no other. "He gets married in two months. Surely…"

"No." His tone brooked no opposition. "He's not going to be allowed to make one more sale. We'll be moving on him immediately. Give it up, Juliette, and be damn glad he was taken down before you could complete this death wish of yours. My God, he'd kill you! You have to know that."

"He'll try." She accepted that risk, as she did all others. "But he won't be able to afford to, at least not at first. The copies I've made of his business records in his various legitimate headquarters will ruin him if they make their way to his rivals' hands." And she'd never quite rid herself of the pang of disappointment that she wouldn't be bringing about his ruination in just that way. To shatter his life on the eve of his wedding and leave him with nothing. But a thief had to be flexible and practical. Sam was right about one thing—it would be enough that the man was brought down.

As long as she got a shot at him first.

"He'll have to play along at first." She lifted a shoulder. "Once he had what he wanted, of course, he'd order my death."

Sam surged to his feet, grasped her upper arms and gave her an ungentle shake. "Are you even listening to yourself?" he demanded, his face shoved close to hers. "Or are you so wrapped up in your damn revenge that you never cared that this plan you're so hellbent on would be a sure way to wind up dead?"

Tossing her head back she met his gaze squarely. "What would you have done in my place?" She knew the question had hit its mark when his expression stilled, his grasp loosened. "If someone you loved was threatened, killed, what would you do to protect them? To avenge them?"

The moment stretched, silence thrumming with emotion. He didn't answer. He didn't need to. She'd seen her answer in the mask of savagery that had flashed across his face. Sam was a warrior, for all his surface civility. She'd witnessed his commitment to his family. He'd do the same as she, or more, to protect one of them.

She played on that emotion now, certain it was her best hope of convincing him. "If your brother hadn't made it, wouldn't you want a piece of the man responsible for putting those bullets in him? Wouldn't you hunt him down, take your revenge one slice at a time, and make sure he knew why he was suffering? That's all I'm asking, Sam. Give me just a little time to finish this with Oppenheimer, and then you can have him." His hard expression was impossible to read. Desperation rose, and she pressed on. "What would it hurt? You get what you want, Oppenheimer behind bars. And I get what I want."

"What's that, a body bag?" He released her with a suddenness that had her stumbling backward. Reaching for his Scotch, he drained the glass, then replaced it on the table with barely restrained violence. "Forget it. You're not thinking clearly.

You've let your hatred of the man blind you to the danger. I'm not going to allow you to have anything further to do with him.''

His words were the surest way to torch her temper. *"You're* not going to allow? I've got news for you, Tremaine, your hold on me is over. I played the game your way, and now you're going to live up to your end of things. Once you destroy the file on me, you can go back to whatever it is you do. I'm no longer any concern of yours, remember? What I do now is my business.''

"It's my business if your future plans threaten ours.'' He turned away, jammed his hands in his pockets. "I have every intention of keeping my word. Just not quite yet.''

There was a sound which she first attributed to fury ringing in her ears. It took a moment longer to realize his phone was ringing again. The one that had brought him word of his brother. When he turned to retrieve it, she whirled away, blood pumping with impotent fury. It couldn't end like this, before Oppenheimer knew just who had deprived him of his most prized possessions. Before he saw her, realized that his monstrous actions of the past hadn't gone unpunished. Thoughts of that moment had driven her for ten years. She'd often imagined they were the one thing that gave her grandmother the strength to fight her weakened heart. Despite what the U.S. government had in store for the man, he wouldn't be held accountable for her mother's death. With no body, no evidence, Oppenheimer's action would never be brought to light.

She was going to let him know that one person, at least, had held him responsible.

Sending a glance over her shoulder, she tuned in to Sam's side of the conversation. He had his back to her, and he was asking whoever was on the other end about antibiotics and chances for infection.

Juliette had a moment of concern. Had his brother's condition worsened? And then on the heels of that thought came another. The fact that it hadn't occurred first only underscored the fact that she'd spent too much time in Sam's company. Let him get too close.

Silently, she crossed to pick up her purse from the table. And then kept going, as quickly as she could, out the door.

When Sam strolled into the safe house he made sure none of the dangerous emotion roiling around inside him showed. As he entered the living room, he took a savage bit of satisfaction at the way Juliette's gaze widened, her lips parting. "Well, this is cozy."

"Tremaine." Miles didn't bother to get up from where he was ensconced on the couch, sitting a bit closer than necessary to her. "A bit careless of you to let her get away from you, wasn't it?"

Careless. There was a word, Sam thought grimly, as he took up position leaning against the opposite wall. It had been careless to lower his guard with her, even for a moment. He knew damn well the lengths she was willing to go to implement her plans. But it had been more reckless to start to care, even a little. To be concerned that the woman seemingly wouldn't be satisfied until she'd destroyed herself in her quest to ruin Oppenheimer. That mistake was unforgivable.

"Didn't take me long to trail her here, did it?" The fact that she'd managed to slip out at all would continue to sting. So her expression at his words provided a slight balm to the ego.

"You didn't follow me," she said, with the certainty of someone who'd covered her tracks. "You couldn't have."

"Tracking device," he explained laconically. He watched the storm brew in her eyes. "I could pinpoint your location exactly from miles away." Actually the device had a far greater range than that, but he was gentleman enough not to rub it in.

"That's how you followed me to Copenhagen!"

Because he knew it would annoy her, he allowed himself a satisfied smile. Then, switching his attention to Miles, he said, "She doesn't figure into this anymore, so I'll take her off your hands."

"On the contrary." Giving the crease of his trousers careful attention, Miles crossed one knee over the other. "I think Ms. Morrow can still be of some help to us."

The words hit him with the force of a punch. "We don't need her help. We have everything necessary to move on Oppenheimer. One phone call and he can be in custody within hours."

"That's true." The look on Caladesh's face said he was enjoying this. "But what if we could get more? What if we could actually find his latest shipment of weapons before he sells them?"

"Is that what she's told you?" He sent a quick glance to Juliette. "Very imaginative." His attention returned to his colleague and his voice hardened. "If she said that she knows where his storage is, she's lying to you, Miles. All she wants is some time to go ahead with her own plans for Oppenheimer, and probably screw up our arrest in the process. We can't afford to wait around while she plays her games. She could end up alerting him and send him into hiding, did you ever think of that?''

The other man withdrew a cigarette, lit it. ''I believe it's worth the risk. From the information in that file it's clear that he moves his freight by water. It makes sense that he'd have an unloading spot, a place where he can store the weapons while he fills his orders and ships them out again.''

''A possibility struck me on the way over here.'' There was an entreaty in her eyes that he chose to ignore. ''My grandmother's family had a summer home on a small island in the Mediterranean. It's isolated there, at least it was when we visited fifteen years ago. We know it didn't get sold, because the taxes are still paid each year in her real name.'' Despite himself, Sam felt his interest sharpening. Tax records would have been easy enough for them to check out, privately and discreetly. ''We couldn't claim it, of course, without alerting Oppenheimer to our whereabouts. It's possible he kept the place for his own purposes.''

''Like smuggling weapons aboard his specially made yacht and storing them near the home,'' Miles put in smoothly. He drew on the cigarette, exhaled a narrow plume of smoke. ''The possibility is too good to miss out on, Sam.''

It took physical effort to release the fist that curled at his side, to keep his voice even. ''A possibility is all it is, and a remote one at that. There's no reason we can't have Oppenheimer picked up first, then check this out.''

"And take the chance of alerting any partners or employees that might have orders to move the shipment?" Miles shook his head. "It's worth this calculated risk. Juliette has agreed to arrange a meeting with the man on the island. And how could he resist a confrontation with *le petit voleur?*" He patted Juliette's knee, an action that didn't escape Sam's notice. Nor did he fail to observe the way his hand lingered there. "She can provide directions to the place. While she's keeping him busy, you can be checking out the island for the weapon store."

"Juliette, would you excuse us for a moment?" His request seemed to take both of them by surprise. Miles looked as though he'd protest, but then she rose, strode out of the room with her head held high. He waited until the door shut behind her before he shoved away from the wall and approached the couch. "What the hell are you after here?"

Caladesh brushed an imaginary piece of lint from his pants. "I'd think that would be clear."

Frustration surged, but Sam tamped it down. It wouldn't do him any good to lose his temper with the man. That wasn't the way to make him see reason. "What's clear to me is that you should have already contacted the Vienna station and told the Chief of Station what we found in that file. After that, it's out of our hands. He'll contact the Austrian Intel and the State Police there will make the arrest. You can't tell me that Headquarters didn't explain that to you very clearly when they called."

"I think you're being a bit shortsighted here." Miles stubbed his cigarette out with movements jerky with agitation. "Have you considered what this could do for both our careers if the store happens to be on that island and we can arrange for its confiscation? My God, man, we'd be heroes. With the number of terrorist groups targeting Americans these days, we're almost assured that these arms are heading to one of them, did you ever think of that? Where's your sense of duty?''

''It's pretty damn clear where yours is,'' Sam shot back. He half turned, fought for control. Caladesh was so blinded by his own ambition that he didn't care about anyone else. The risk wasn't his, after all. He wouldn't be the one investigating that island. And he sure as hell wouldn't be the one confronting Oppenheimer.

The thought of Juliette doing just that made a cold sweat break out on his forehead. There were so many things that could go wrong he'd need a book to list them all. But the first and most serious danger was that to Juliette. He swung around, found that Miles had risen.

''I think I can sell this to Headquarters, as long as we move quickly.''

Sam gave an incredulous laugh. Given the spin Miles was likely to put on it, he had no doubt the man was right. ''Have you bothered to give a thought to Juliette's safety in this scheme? I can't be two places at once, searching the island and keeping watch on her with Oppenheimer.''

''I have faith in you.'' Miles's shrug was indifferent. ''At any rate, should things start going wrong, you're to get the hell out of there. She's expendable.''

He didn't plan his next action. There was just a roaring in his ears, a red mist hazing his vision as he plowed a fist into the man's face, snapping his head back. A vicious blade of satisfaction sliced through him when he saw the blood pour from Miles's nose. "Expendable? Is that the way you think of your contacts?"

"Tremaine, you crazy bastard!" the man moaned, both his hands coming up to dam the blood rushing down his face. "What the hell's wrong with you?" He fumbled for his handkerchief, brought it to his face as he muttered curses. He glared at Sam over the top of it. "If I could, I'd have you replaced right now. Your objectivity is compromised. This is going in my report. All of it. My God, man, she's just a common thief!"

His fist throbbed with a satisfying ache. Sam flexed his fingers and couldn't summon an ounce of regret. "She's *my* thief. And there's nothing common about her." He turned to exit the room, his strides eating up the area. Pausing at the door, he looked back over his shoulder. The other man had sunk onto the couch with his head tipped back.

"Oh, and Miles?" He waited for the man's gaze to meet his, then bared his teeth. "I think we both know what you can do with your report."

Chapter 13

"I wish you'd relax. Nothing will go wrong." Juliette had to lean over to speak right into Sam's ear. Conversation was difficult over the noise of the unmarked helicopter's rotors.

He slid her a glance, which was as much attention as she'd gotten from him for the past thirty-six hours. "If there's one thing I've learned from these operations, it's that anything can go wrong, and does."

The truth in his statement was hard to refute. And her own experiences would back it up. She tried to plan for every contingency before she went on a job, but unexpected complications could arise. A guard could vary his routine; equipment could malfunction; an escape route could be blocked. But those were eventualities that could be overcome. It was almost impossible to predict this upcoming meeting with Oppenheimer.

A tattoo of anticipation was beating in her veins.

The man at her side had made no secret of his vehement disapproval of this plan. But when Miles, sporting a swollen nose and surly attitude, had announced that he'd received approval for it, there was little Sam could do but grimly join in mapping out the details.

The speed with which it was happening was dizzying. Before she'd met Sam, before he'd set her schedule awry, she'd thought she had another two months to gradually escalate the ruination of Oppenheimer.

Any disappointment she felt that her plans had taken such an abrupt detour was tempered by the realization that she was finally going to confront him. He'd know who'd been targeting him all these years, and why. And she'd stand before him secure in the knowledge that despite the fact that he'd never be held responsible for her mother's death, he would lose it all. Perhaps not completely by her hands, but it would be enough. It had to be enough.

"Undo your shirt." The words had her gaze whipping to Sam's. But there was nothing suggestive in his eyes. They were still flat, hard and more than a little condemning. "I want to wire you so I can keep track of what's going on between you and Oppenheimer while I'm taking a look around."

"I'll probably be searched," she objected, even as her hands went to the first button.

"At the very least," he agreed tersely. "But they won't find this." As she unfastened her shirt he reached in to withdraw something from his pack. Without preamble he pushed her hands aside and pulled down one of her bra straps.

Shock held her rigid. But again there was nothing

in the least loverlike in his touch. He slipped his
fingers inside the top of her bra and attached a miniscule object close, very close, to her nipple. Unlike
his completely impersonal touch, her own body was
reacting. Her breast tingled where his knuckles
rubbed against it, the nipple drawing up into a hard,
tight knot.

Embarrassed by her involuntary response, especially in the face of his lack of one, she blurted out,
"What's it connected to?"

"It's a wireless transmitter. I'll be wearing the receiver. If you get into trouble, I'll know."

She went still. "You can't afford to divide your
attention worrying about me. There's bound to be
guards all over the place. We're both professionals.
Let's agree that we each take care of ourselves."

"It's your game, Juliette." There was no mistaking the bitterness in his tone. "But we're playing it
by my rules." He tested the security of the microphone, then, seemingly satisfied, withdrew his fingers. The skin he'd so recently warmed abruptly
chilled. He couldn't have stated any more clearly his
opposition to this plan. He didn't need to. She'd
heard all his arguments earlier. And knowing that
they were primarily fueled by worry for her made a
heavy knot of guilt twist through her stomach.

She couldn't afford the feeling. She hadn't asked
for his concern, she told herself shakily, fingers re-
doing her buttons. Had never wanted to elicit that
kind of response from any man. Emotions were a
sticky tangle best left to others. Focus on a goal demanded single-minded attention. Distraction could
prove fatal. She didn't know what to do with his

concern, in any case. She was unused to offering it. Even more unused to receiving it.

He diverted her then by going over instructions again. She pretended to listen, although he'd repeated them at least twenty times. The small flat radio she could use to communicate with the pilot was in one shoe, a case with a slim lethal blade was in the other. She didn't need him to point out that she was walking in less prepared and in more danger than she'd ever faced before. She knew that, and accepted the risk. Embraced it.

Her gaze went to the map lit up next to the pilot's controls. They were getting close. And the moment she'd been waiting for loomed. The outline of the island was below them, lights glowing in what had to be the house. There had been other homes on the island the one time she'd visited it, but there were no other lights to be seen. If Oppenheimer were using the island as a transition point for smuggled weapons, it would be imperative to have complete privacy. He'd have bought the other homeowners out.

Sam leaned over her, night-vision binoculars to his face. "No gate. No guards in the open, at least."

"He'll have them hidden somewhere," she replied certainly. "He won't have obeyed my order to come alone. He'll feel secure surrounded by his own men." Memory of the phone call when she'd given him those orders still had the power to satisfy. She'd let him think she was calling for *le petit voleur,* passing on the thief's demands for this meeting. He'd been disbelieving, then, when she'd listed everything she'd stolen from him over the years, apoplectic. But she'd never doubted that he'd accede, at least to the meeting. After what she'd told him, he'd be too afraid not to.

The helicopter dropped altitude, circling the house in smaller and smaller arcs until it was directly before it. "How's this?" the pilot shouted over his shoulder.

Sam peered out, the binoculars still to his face. "Looks like as good a place as any." When he turned back to her, she was already reaching for the hook to the harness she wore around her chest. Taking it from her, he fastened it for her, then shoved the door open.

Juliette went to the doorway and crouched, balancing on the balls of her feet as she'd been instructed. Heights held no fear for her. She was used to rappelling up and down walls on cables thinner than the one that would hold her now. The thin leather gloves would protect her hands. Poised, she readied to jump.

"Wait."

Impatient, she turned her head. Sam leaned in, shoved his hand in her hair and pulled her face toward his. The kiss was hard, rough and over too quickly. When he drew away, there was a hollow place in her stomach, as if her freefall into space had already taken place.

"Be careful."

She read the words on his lips. "You, too," she whispered, forcing herself to turn away. Grasping the cable in both hands, she drew in a breath and then leaped. There was a euphoric sensation of flying, of soaring through the air. She began to slide down the cable, arms straining with effort. She could have allowed it to lower her down from the hook on her harness, but she was unwilling to give up even that one small bit of control.

The ground seemed to rush up at her, then her feet hit it, hard enough to have her jaw snapping shut with real force. She unsnapped the hook so it could be drawn back up into the helicopter. She never noticed when the chopper started moving away. Her attention was on the house twenty yards away from her, the door still firmly shut.

From the little she could detect in the dark, the villa hadn't changed much since the one time she'd seen it. The sculpted white Provençal stone gleamed in the night, and it sprawled across the area with a kind of majestic indolence. She didn't get more than a dozen steps before she heard the sound of running footsteps behind her. Juliette wasn't surprised to feel rough hands haul her backward to a halt. Nor to feel the pressure of a cool metal barrel against her temple.

"Monsieur Oppenheimer m'attend."

"C'est une femme!"

The guard's surprise at finding she was a woman, didn't have him lowering his gun. She was pushed unceremoniously up the marble steps, toward the polished mahogany door, which was swinging open.

Oppenheimer stood there, the light spilling behind him in an unholy glow. He was dressed totally in white, his shirt open part way to reveal a heavy gold chain around his throat. All the oxygen leeched from her lungs. She'd seen him over the years, of course. From a distance. Enough to note that the strong build and barrel chest had begun to soften, to run to fat. He'd grown bald, his brown hair thinned to a fringe that ran from ear to ear. An all too familiar ripple of revulsion was skating down her spine. Anxious to deny it, she straightened her shoulders. The time had long passed when she'd let this man terrify her. Or intimidate her.

The frown on his round face deepened to a scowl as Juliette was shoved to stop before him. *"Où est-il?"*

"Where is whom?" she answered in English. By the arrested look on his face, she knew he'd recognized her voice from her earlier phone call. "I promised you a meeting with *le petit voleur*. And here I am."

There was silence for a moment as he considered her words. A moment in which she held her breath, wondering if he could possibly recognize her from ten years ago. Then he gave a snort, barked out an order to the man beside her. *"Recherchez-la."*

The guard ran his hands roughly over her form, chest to ankle. With a shake of his head, he stepped back.

"Do you expect me to believe that the most notorious thief on the continent is a woman?" The gold backing on his front tooth glinted as he grinned, a lascivious smile that summoned nasty splinters of memory. "And a very lovely woman, at that." His English had improved noticeably in the past decade, she observed. It was the only improvement of note.

She strolled past him, as if admiring the marble floors, the white sweeping staircase. "That's a rather chauvinistic attitude in this day and age, don't you think?"

His expression darkened at the derision in her tone. *"Le petit voleur* must be a coward to allow a woman to do his work for him. Or are you to distract me while he strikes elsewhere? Beautiful as you are,

I'm not so easily fooled.'' He gave another order and the guard hurried away.

Her stomach lurched as she thought of the danger to Sam. As the guards searched the island for the man Oppenheimer was convinced must have accompanied her, they could well run across him as he conducted his search. A shaft of fear arrowed through her at the thought of him being discovered.

''I came alone, didn't I, as we agreed? You did not. Which of us is the coward, I wonder?'' She made no attempt to keep the mockery from her tone. It had the desired effect.

He grabbed her arm, fingers biting into the flesh. ''You'll show me some respect.''

Her gaze battled his, saw the same demon who had destroyed her life. Who had forged it with purpose. ''You never earned that.'' Pulling away from him, she dug in her pocket, flipped the gold coin to him. ''You didn't earn this either, did you? Or the chest full of ingots just like it. Must be hell for a man like you to have them and not let anyone know it. Moira can never wear that sapphire in your vault, either, can she? Someone would be bound to recognize it.''

He stared at the coin in his hand, then at her. ''Where did you get this?''

''You know where I got it.'' Amazingly, she was beginning to enjoy herself. Even in face of the threat, there was a hum of adrenaline in her veins. Senses were heightened. And all of them were focused on him. ''The lockbox it was in is tucked away in the vault on your estate. The one that also houses a rather sizable porn collection.'' She allowed pity to tinge her tone, knowing he'd hate it. ''I have to wonder what kind of man leaves a fiancée thirty years his junior sleeping alone while he entertains himself with skin flicks.'' Her shrug said that he had been judged, and found lacking.

''You're lying,'' he said flatly. ''Nothing was missing from that vault.''

''Really? Then how do you explain that?'' she nodded at the coin clutched tightly in his hand. ''How did I know what you kept inside it?'' She watched the realization flicker across his face, chased by rage. ''Nothing else was missing because I *chose* not to remove it. What you kept is only because I allowed it after I disabled your cameras.'' An ugly flush was crawling up his neck, mottling his face. ''I took care of the dogs. Circumvented the house alarm, entered the house and waited. I was right there when you and your irritable fiancée came in the door, do you know that? I waited for you to finish…whatever it was you did alone in the office.'' With a raise of her brows she intimated exactly what she thought that might have been. ''And while you slept I entered your office, and your vault.''

''You're lying.'' It was rage rather than logic that fueled his words. ''That vault is totally secure.''

''Nothing is secure from *le petit voleur*,'' she said, with more than a little arrogance. ''I would have thought you'd realized that when I snatched the Moonfire. What a pity that you'll never hang it around your fiancée's throat right before she walks down that aisle. But you know what they say about the best-laid plans.''

The wrath in his expression was familiar. And

when his fist arced through the air, catching her on the cheekbone, the shattering pain that followed was all too familiar, as well.

Sam clutched the rock, using the giant stack of boulders to hide him from view. The water lapped around his waist as he shrugged out of the waterproof pack and opened it. He picked up the receiver, fit the earpiece to his ear. The earphones that would allow him to communicate with the pilot were placed around his neck. Right now his first concern was for Juliette. He adjusted the knob on the transmitter, then heard voices, as clearly as if they were coming from next to him. He listened for a moment, a fraction of tension seeping from his limbs. Oppenheimer didn't believe she was the thief who'd robbed him of his most prized possessions. He had no doubt that she'd take great satisfaction in convincing him otherwise.

He reached into the pack, pulled out some night-vision goggles and put them on. After surveying the area carefully, he pushed away from the rocks and waded to shore. Once on dry ground he sat down and exchanged his water shoes for a pair of sneakers. Then he began to make his way to the hulking build-ing they'd spotted from the helicopter, the one hug-ging the shoreline. Although there was another dock on the opposite side of the island, with a large boat moored to it, this was the only other building on the island, with the exception of the villa. If he was go-ing to find anything of significance, it would be in there.

Twice on his way toward it he had to take cover behind a dune, and wait until guards, singly or in pairs, covered the area armed with flashlights and automatics. Once a man walked right by him, so near he could have reached out and touched him. Sam had been ready to act with swift deadly force to take him out, but it hadn't been necessary. The man had passed by.

It took another five minutes to jog to the building. He didn't approach it right away. Instead, he circled it from a distance, spotting the men searching around it. Flattening himself between the dunes again, he reached for the earphones around his neck, spoke into the microphone. "Buzz them across the southwest corner of the island." He waited for the pilot to obey, watched the figures rush to the area beneath the path of the helicopter. Only when he'd assured himself that the two men at the building were headed in that same direction did he advance toward it.

Up close it appeared nothing more sinister than a boathouse, albeit a large one. A yacht the size of Oppenheimer's would never be able to dock at the large pier leading from the building, but a fairly good-size seaworthy ship would. Despite himself, he felt a spark of excitement, one he immediately tamped down. Even if Juliette's hunch paid off, it didn't excuse the risk they were taking. The danger she was deliberately placing herself in.

He was a man who knew the high price of honor. Of loyalty and devotion. He'd operated by such a code all his life. He hadn't expected to discover that the thief who'd been targeting Oppenheimer for years operated according to her own code. More than money had motivated her. More than greed. Revenge wasn't a pretty emotion, nor a tame one. But it was one he could empathize with. When she'd recounted her story about her life with Oppenheimer, he'd felt a burn of rage unlike anything he'd ever experienced before. He knew what he'd be capable of if someone he loved was threatened. And despite his fear for her safety, he couldn't judge her for the thirst that drove her. The desire for revenge could be a cruel mistress. He just hoped it didn't prove to be a lethal one.

Stealthily, he flattened himself against the building, and slid along the side. A quick surveillance of the perimeter of the steel structure proved there were no windows. The only opening was the huge set of double sliding doors. He took out a metal wand, similar to the one Juliette had used on the estate, and checked the doors for security. He wasn't totally surprised to find none. The isolation of the island worked in Oppenheimer's favor. And there was no doubt that even if the island was breached, the guards with automatic weapons strapped to their chests were a powerful deterrent in their own right.

There was a heavy chain and padlock securing the doors shut. He was tempted to use the bolt cutter, but decided to expend the extra time and energy picking the lock. A guard could be forgiven for believing someone had been careless enough to leave the doors unlocked, but a cut chain would signal for sure that security had been breached.

With a pencil flashlight held between his teeth, he worked as quickly as he could, but he lacked Juliette's level of expertise. It took longer than it should have to open the padlock and slip inside.

The interior was vast, and dark as a cave. Sweeping the flashlight's slim beam around the area, he saw that the back of the space was stacked high with crates. The structure must have served to store a large boat at one time. Water sloshed beneath the walkways. But the back of the area rested on land. He was heading toward the area when he heard Juliette's voice in his ear, followed by an unmistakable sound.

He stopped short in his tracks, rage leaping through his veins. Oppenheimer had struck her. His fists clenched inside the thin latex gloves he wore. For a moment, just one, he allowed himself the indulgence of imagining his fingers around the other man's throat, squeezing tightly. There would be a certain savage satisfaction in making him pay for laying his hands on Juliette. In making him pay for all the suffering he'd brought to her.

He heard her voice again, steady, mocking the man. It took more effort than it should have to uncurl his fists. To move toward the crates. Time and again she'd proved her ability to take care of herself. But her skill in that area didn't prevent him from wanting to shield her from risk. From hurt. Grimly, he recognized one truth Miles had uttered. Sam had lost his objectivity, at least where she was concerned. He could no longer deny it. Nor could he bring himself to care.

"Still hitting women, Hans?" Lances of pain radiated from her cheekbone. She almost welcomed the ache. It banished any remaining trepidation, and left only resolve in its wake. "I'm not surprised. You always were a spineless bully. Which angers you most, I wonder? The fact that I have the Moonfire, or the fact that I broke into your estate." She cupped her hand to her cheek, feeling the heat that still lingered there and gave him a taunting smile. "You're not thinking clearly. If you were, you'd be wondering where else I've slipped in and out of without you knowing. And what reasons I might have had for doing so.''

''I'll kill you where you stand.'' His voice trembled with fury. ''What will that damn thief think when his messenger's body is found floating in the Seine?''

''That would be exceedingly shortsighted of you, considering that over the years I've accessed nearly every corporate headquarters in which you have an interest. It's convenient to have those legitimate fronts to cover the income derived from your other activities, isn't it?'' She waited for awareness to flicker across his face, followed by wariness. ''I have copies of documents that your rivals would find very interesting. Not to mention the authorities.'' Her smile was rapier sharp. ''Touch me again, and those documents will be used to destroy you.''

It took more courage than it should have to walk past him, relying on memory to guide her through the home. To her left was an airy room with vaulted ceilings and white pillars dotting the area. Selecting a chair, she sat, crossed her legs.

''You're lying. About all of it. A woman isn't capable of the jobs *le petit voleur* has pulled.''

He'd followed her into the room. She understood that by not sitting he was establishing his power, making her tilt her head up to look at him. He'd always been quite well versed in ways to control people. But he wasn't going to be allowed to control her, or this situation.

''Really? I've found that people are capable of anything, given the right motivation. I wanted to strip you of everything you cared about, and I've managed nicely, haven't I? I understand that the insurance companies quit issuing you coverage." She didn't attempt to keep the smugness from her voice. "That was a side benefit I hadn't expected. And now I'm going to destroy you with the information I've stolen unless you pay me quite an impressive sum of money. I can assure you I'm quite *capable* of following through. Where you're concerned, I'm capable of just about anything."

"Why?" he asked bluntly. His face had settled into a stoic mask that revealed none of the rage she knew he was feeling. "Why me? There are dozens of richer men on the continent."

There was a burning in her belly, fueled by a wealth of bitterness. "Have you made so many enemies, Hans, that you can't recall any single one that might wish you harm?" He stilled, stared hard at her. "It's true I could have targeted anyone I chose, if money was all I was after. But revenge is so much more personal, don't you think? And although it's been ten years in the planning, I must say, I've found it every bit as fulfilling as I could have hoped."

He stared at her for several moments, as comprehension mingled with disbelief on his countenance.

Settling farther back in her chair, she plucked at the black trousers she wore, feigning disappointment. "Still having trouble with your memory? A woman doesn't like to believe she's that forgettable. It's been a decade since I escaped from your penthouse. But you surely must have wondered how I knew about this place." She paused a beat. "I'm sure you'll understand why Grandmama failed to send her love."

"Alison?" The word seemed to have been torn from his throat. He did sit then, a graceless drop to the seat behind him as he continued to gape at her.

"I see you do remember me." Her throat was clogged with emotion, her chest tight with it. Old grief, she discovered, could still throb like a fresh wound. "So I'm certain you also remember my mother."

Chapter 14

The back of the boathouse was cluttered with tools strewn next to the stacks of crates. Whatever the boxes held, it was obvious they were opened here. Selecting a crowbar, Sam climbed the shortest stack and fought to find a secure foothold while he worked. The pencil flashlight clenched between his teeth, he wielded the tool on the lid of the top one. Given his awkward position, it took longer than expected. When he'd loosened the top, he moved it over to the next stack, and dug through the foam fill for the contents beneath.

His search yielded an object wrapped in heavy plastic. He knew by touch alone that it wasn't a weapon. Tearing aside enough of the covering to identify the object, he found a delicate urn, covered with Eastern markings. Although he didn't doubt it would fetch a high price in a trendy store, it was obviously new. And just as obviously not what he was looking for.

Hissing out a breath, he shifted position enough to set it on top of the lid he'd removed, and lifted out another. And then another. There were a dozen of them in all, in two layers, and despite what he knew about some of the endeavors the man was involved in, the shipping of overpriced knickknacks wasn't a crime.

A small noise sounded in the confines of the building. Straining his ears, Sam waited for it to be repeated. When it was, he relaxed a bit, satisfied that it was just a vigorous wave slapping against a mooring. Turning back toward the opened crate, he started the task of repacking it. He'd set the first of the urns carefully inside before stopping when his knuckles scraped the bottom of the crate.

He paused, leaned back precariously from his perch to examine the exterior of it. With his hand still inside, he rapped on the side of the crate where it ended, measured the distance visually. It was a good eighteen inches above the bottom edge of the box.

Excitement began to thrum through his veins. It wouldn't make sense to add another wood slat merely to protect another layer of urns. He took the vase out that he'd been replacing and reached for the crowbar again. The foam impeded his progress, but when he got one corner loosened he set the instrument aside. Wrenching upward with both hands, he had the false bottom off and was staring at the contents nestled beneath.

Machine guns. He leaned closer, so the beam of the flashlight would provide better illumination.

M-60E3s, from the looks of them. The weapons were routinely used by the U.S. counterterrorist teams. With a grim sort of irony, he realized that thanks to Oppenheimer, some of the terrorist groups the U.S. battled would be as well-equipped as the American teams.

Upon the heels of that realization, came another. This discovery meant the mission here had been accomplished. There was no reason to linger on the island any longer. A sense of urgency began to build. Oppenheimer wasn't going to risk his cache of weapons being discovered. And unless Juliette was very, very convincing, he wasn't going to believe it was a coincidence she'd insisted on meeting here.

He reached for the mike attached to the earphones around his neck. Tersely, he instructed the pilot to radio Miles with the find. If Caladesh acted quickly, local law enforcement would soon be swarming over this island.

Adjusting the transmitter he wore, he listened for a moment to Juliette's voice as he returned to the task of repacking the crate. His hands faltered when he heard her expose her identity to the man. Others might not hear the pain that threaded her words. Might not guess at the weight she'd carried around for far too long. He couldn't prevent a reaction to both. With an odd sense of resignation, he accepted that she'd begun to matter to him. More than was comfortable for a man whose life revolved around commitment only to his immediate family and to his country. The time was fast approaching when he was going to have to decide how to deal with that. And how to get Juliette to deal with it, as well.

Working quickly, he replaced all the urns, shoving

aside handfuls of foam to cover them. He set the lid down on top of the crate as securely as he could. With any luck, the island would be overrun by law enforcement personnel before the crate could be discovered.

Taking the flashlight in his hand, he climbed down the stack of crates and headed toward the door again. When Juliette heard the chopper overhead, that would be her cue to wrap things up with Oppenheimer. While she was safely boarding the helicopter, he'd be swimming back to the location where he'd been dropped earlier. If their luck continued to hold, they'd be on their way back to Paris within the next twenty minutes.

Slipping from the building would be tricky. He listened, but couldn't hear a sound outside. In the time it took him to push the door open and slip outside, he'd be totally exposed if one of the guards had returned. He didn't draw the gun he had snugged at the small of his back. He needed his hands free to refasten the chain and padlock.

He slipped through the door and secured it. He crept to the corner of the building, carefully peered around it. There was no one in sight, although he could hear voices drifting along the water. The guards were continuing their search.

He headed in the opposite direction, intent on finding a place to take cover until the chopper got there. With considerable effort, he focused his attention off the drama that was playing out between Juliette and Oppenheimer. The next few minutes until he got her safely off the island were going to be the most grueling of his career.

Instinct alerted him even before he heard the small

sound behind him. Throwing himself to the side, he reached for his gun at the same time. He hit the ground, rolled once and came to his feet in a crouch, weapon drawn. And found himself looking up at the barrels of two assault rifles, both of which were pointed at his head.

He didn't need to translate the command uttered by one of the guards to know enough to drop his weapon. Hands half-raised, he rose slowly. With his weight poised on the balls of his feet he waited for them to flank him, order him on the ground. Feigning confusion, he said haltingly, *"Je ne parle pas français."* One of the men moved closer to shove him down and when he did, Sam sprang.

Yanking him off balance, he knocked the gun barrel aside and twisted his body, using the man as a human shield as he rushed the other guard. The impact of bodies colliding sounded extra loud in the stillness. One rifle went flying when Sam sent an uppercut to the man's jaw. The second guard was aiming again when Sam used the first man's body to shove him off balance. With a well-placed kick he doubled the man over. The weapon slipped out of his grasp as he gagged and dropped to his knees, clutching his genitals with both hands.

The first guard knocked Sam to the ground, and they rolled, engaged in a near silent lethal battle. The other man ended up on top, and his hands wrapped around Sam's throat, squeezing tightly. Sam landed a punch that had the guard's head snapping back, but his grip didn't loosen appreciably. His head was lifted to be slammed against the ground. Colors dancing before his eyes, he knew consciousness was receding quickly. Making a bridge of his hand, he drove it sharply upward, catching the guard beneath his nose. There was a sickening crunch of bone giving way and the other man's grasp grew lax, as his limbs went boneless.

Shoving the body off him, Sam stumbled to his feet, nearly fell. The first guard was attempting to rise as well. Sam picked up the rifle and drove the butt sharply into the side of the man's head. Swaying slightly, he surveyed the two unconscious bodies. He had no idea how many of the guards were on the island, or how soon it would be before these two were missed. But he did know that his and Juliette's luck had abruptly run out.

It took valuable minutes to search his pack for a length of nylon rope to tie the men together. Even more time to rip the sleeves from their shirts, to use them as gags. Tossing one rifle into the water, he slipped the strap of the other over his neck. Then he dragged them to the edge of the dock and pushed them off. The water wasn't deep enough to drown them, but their location would ensure that no one stumbled over them for a bit. Hopefully it would buy him enough time to get Juliette off the island without more trouble.

Juliette. For the first time he became aware that he'd lost the transmitter that kept him connected to her. Swearing, he went back to the scene of the struggle with the guards. He found the goggles first. He must have dropped them when he'd rolled across the ground. With their aid he was able to locate the transmitter. He picked it up and fitted it into his ear even as he jogged for cover. The faint whir of the chopper could be heard in the distance. It wouldn't be long now.

Ducking between a couple dunes, he adjusted the transmitter for a clearer reception. What he heard had every muscle in his body going tense, ice shooting up his spine. There were definite sounds of a struggle going on in the villa. Even as the realization occurred, he heard Juliette cry out, as if in pain. The sound propelled him forward. He ran toward the villa in a crouch. The noise from the transmitter couldn't drown out the scream of panic blazing across his mind.

He couldn't be too late. He couldn't be.

Juliette stared at Oppenheimer with burning eyes. Old bitterness had festered, erupted, an oozing open sore. "You do remember Celeste, don't you? Or have you murdered so many women you can't keep them all straight?"

He'd recovered admirably from the shock of discovering her identity. Even now he was looking her up and down with unmistakable avarice. "Little Alison. You grew up nicely, in spite of everything. You have the look of Celeste in your eyes. Although I never recall hers looking quite as dangerous as yours do right now."

"I am dangerous," she said softly. His use of her real name was barely familiar, as if it belonged to a passing acquaintance she'd known long, long ago. Alison London had died ten years ago, and Juliette Morrow had been born in her place. Tremors of fury were racking her system. "I'm the woman who's made it her life's work to make you pay for every thing you ever did to us. Do you think the cost has been high so far? It's going to get far greater. If I release those records the authorities will descend on your businesses with magnifying glasses. Any hint of wrongdoing in any of them and you'll be tied up in the courts for years.''

"My businesses are legitimate.'' He reached up, adjusted his collar. The gold insignia ring on his finger winked in the lamplight. Her attention was drawn to it, held. She knew without closer examination that it was fashioned into a crest, a twisted dragon with rubies for eyes. In her mind she could still see the glint of it on his hand, as his fingers ripped her blouse from her young form.

Nausea rose, threatened to choke her. Ruthlessly, she turned her back on the young, vulnerable fourteen-year-old she'd been. All that mattered now was that she finish this. Finish him. She managed a nonchalant shrug. "You may be right. Your business rivals may find the documents of more interest. Especially the ones disclosing your practices of bribing your competitors' employees to engage in corporate espionage for you.'' She saw with satisfaction that she'd scored a direct hit.

"I want twenty million dollars wired to my private account. Once the transaction has taken place, the copies of your documents will be returned, and I'll stop targeting your property.'' She gave him a taunting smile. "I've been thinking of retiring, but I'll need a nest egg. Living expenses can be so unreasonable.'' He'd understand a demand for money. He'd expect it. And before he could inevitably begin plotting how to get his hands on the copied documents, while having her eliminated, he'd be in prison. For a moment she could almost be satisfied with that.

"You dare to blackmail me? Me?'' His fingers

were curled into tight fists of rage. "I could have you killed before you walk out this door."

"Murder?" She lifted her brow. "Not exactly unfamiliar territory for you, is it?"

"They never found your mother's body, did they?"

She swallowed hard, struggled to remain impassive. But he pressed on, as if aware he'd drawn blood. "I'm afraid I had to insist she participate in one of my films. After my instruction, she certainly had the aptitude for it."

She froze, Sam's words echoing in her mind. *I'd heard he started out in the porn field.*

As if reading her thoughts, he continued. "Isn't it ironic that her debut film was also her denouement? She played her part quite well. Right up to her untimely end. Had you known, you could have found a copy in my collection in the vault."

An awful truth began to register, was violently rejected. For a moment Juliette thought she'd be ill. His voice faded in and out, each sentence flaying away a bit more of the last illusion she had remaining. There was a name for the type of pornography that featured an all too final ending for one of the participants. And the horrible thought of her mother meeting her death that way had a hot ball of grief and fury surging through her.

"I've changed my mind," she said, getting to her feet. Her knees were so weak that for a moment she wondered if they'd hold her. "We'll make it thirty million. You can afford it, and God knows you deserve far worse." She didn't even attempt to keep the emotion from her voice. She wasn't that good an actress. "I'll call you tomorrow with the account number. Once the money has been transferred, we'll talk again.''

She wasn't allowed two steps before he'd surged to his feet, grabbed her arm. When he wrenched it behind her, a startled cry of pain escaped her. ''Do you think I'm just going to let you walk out of here?'' His laugh was ugly. ''I'd expect even Celeste's child to be more intelligent than that.''

There was a primitive part of her that wanted to punish him for even speaking her mother's name. But another, cooler part knew what she had to do to extricate herself. ''Then you'll be impressed to know that a contact of mine has orders to distribute those documents if I don't return unharmed.''

His grip grew tighter. ''If there is a contact, you can be made to reveal the name. To make the call and say whatever I tell you.''

He was too close. His proximity was eliciting old memories she was usually more successful at shoving aside. The last time he'd been this close, he'd nearly raped her. And she'd vowed she'd never cower before this man again. Never be held helpless and weak.

She'd never be his victim.

The hard jab she sent in his gut was rewarded by a single vicious slap. Juliette let her weight go limp, reaching for the weapon in her shoe. At that moment Oppenheimer let her go, dropped down beside her, his hands tearing at her shirt.

And then the villa abruptly went dark.

She toed her shoe off as she struggled with him, heard the knife go skidding across the floor. Drawing her knee up, she struck hard at him, rolling away after she made contact. Her hand made a blind sweep across the floor, fingers searching for the weapon. Before she could reach it he landed on her from behind, straddled her.

"I think you're in desperate need of some of the lessons your mother needed to learn." He shoved a hand up the front of her shirt, groped her breast. "Let's hope you're a better pupil."

Revulsion and remembered fear took over. Logic was impossible to summon. Juliette was a creature of instinctive emotion now, reacting to the threat that had haunted her dreams for far too long. She stretched, muscles straining, felt the plastic sheathe that encased the knife.

There was a tiny click. That was the first inkling she had that she wasn't alone in the room with Oppenheimer any longer. Even as she inched the weapon closer, she looked up and over her shoulder.

Sam stood there, an avenging angel in warrior guise. The relief that flooded her at the sight of him made her muscles go weak. He had a rifle pointed at the man on top of her, and there was a merciless edge to his voice when he spoke. "If you get off her, right now, I just might allow you to live."

"Easy." Oppenheimer's soothing tone immediately had tension reflooding her system. "I'm sure we can work this out."

She didn't trust his capitulation. Reaching farther, she slid the knife toward her, just as she felt the man's arm go beneath her throat, the other shoving her head around in a painful position.

"I'll break her neck before you get a round off. Do you want to take that chance?" His voice rose. "Drop the weapon. Slide it over here."

Fear sprinted up her spine as Sam slowly lowered

the rifle. Neither of them stood a chance if Oppenheimer disarmed him. And while she'd been willing to take such a risk before she'd come in, everything inside her rebelled at the thought of Sam having to pay that kind of price.

She moved the knife closer. The sheathe was removed. And in one fierce movement she drove the blade deep into the arm that still gripped her throat. He cursed in pain. She pulled the blade out as Sam raised the rifle and clubbed him with the butt. The blow drove the man sideways and Juliette moved in a flash, following him over until her knee was on his chest, the tip of the blade beneath his chin.

"I've waited for this moment for ten years," she said, her voice shaking. There was a light of fear in the man's eyes. It filled her with exultant satisfaction. Had there been a similar light in her mother's eyes moments before the life had flickered out of them for good? Her hand trembled, pressed harder, breaking the skin. A drop of blood dripped down the blade. Then another.

"We can make a deal," Oppenheimer said. His face was sheened in sweat. With the smell of fear on him he didn't resemble a monster at all, but merely a pitiful excuse for a human being. "That twenty million? It's yours. Just leave me the account number. For God's sake…" His eyes bulged as the knife pressed deeper. "I can make things right. Give me a chance."

"Did you give my mother a chance?" She didn't recognize the harshness of her own voice. Didn't recognize the sly whisper inside that urged her to act, to drive the blade deeper. Who would miss the man? Who would blame her?

"Juliette." Sam's voice sounded as if from a distance. Slowly, jerkily, she looked up at him. Then heard the sound of the chopper's rotors, the shout of men. "Finish it, one way or another. Time's running out."

Finish it. Her gaze held his, unspoken understanding between them. Make a choice. Allow the man to live or die. And whatever her decision, make peace with it.

Her attention returned to Oppenheimer. She increased the pressure on the knife, watched the panic flood his face.

Then just as abruptly, she relinquished the pressure, and rose. "Let's go."

"Hold this."

Startled, she turned to Sam in time to take the rifle he handed her. Then he reached down and grabbed Oppenheimer's shirt, hauling the man upward. He slammed a fist into his face, once, then again.

"They're coming!" Steps could be heard running toward the house. Sam looked up. The stamp of brutal savagery on his features had her catching her breath. With one final blow he let the man drop to the floor, stood and grabbed her hand. "Where's the back door?"

She led him through the house. They burst out the back door even as the front slammed open. Sam scattered the guards in the area with a round of rifle fire. The helicopter was nowhere in sight, but she could hear it nearby. Sam was pulling her toward the shoreline, where a ship was tied to the dock.

Bullets kicked up the dirt beside them as they ran. "Can you swim?"

His question seemed almost surreal, given the circumstances. "When I have to."

He stopped, took aim, and fired at the boat. A moment later the gas tank exploded, the sound ripping through the night. A huge fireball arose from it. Then he turned, pushed her past the burning boat and into the water. "Tonight you have to."

"I just cannot believe it's over." Juliette's grandmother sat in the penthouse without her usual impeccable posture, looking every bit her eighty years. "And Oppenheimer…" She looked from Sam to Juliette. "He is in custody?"

"He's in jail while the Austrian and French police quibble over him," Sam answered. He stretched his legs out, crossed the ankles. A bone-deep weariness was beginning to make its way through his muscles. "There are enough charges in each country to assure that he spends the rest of his life in prison. Illegal arms sales are taken seriously. And the proof that he's been arming terrorists will seal his fate." He was suspected of far more than he'd ever have to account for. The agency was still trying to establish a link between him and the deaths of the Brunei royal family that had taken place last year. And according to the last conversation Miles had relayed from Headquarters, the body of Sterling, the case officer who'd betrayed both Sam and his contract agent to Oppenheimer, had just washed up on a Brazilian beach. They lacked the evidence to hang any of those deaths on the man, although there was no doubt of his guilt.

His gaze went to Juliette, where she stood with her hand resting comfortingly on her grandmother's shoulder. With the statements the man had made about Celeste, and the copy of the film that was attained from his vault, there still might be a way to hold him responsible for the woman's death. He was going to do his damnedest to try.

Pauline reached up, clutched Juliette's hand. "Did you...did he tell you what happened to your mother?"

She looked at Sam, an unspoken message in her eyes. "No, Grandmama. He never admitted to anything."

Silently, he commended her action. There were worse things than not knowing. Juliette had discovered that for herself. He couldn't blame her for wanting to spare her grandmother. He listened while she gave the woman a greatly abbreviated version of their adventure the previous night. She glossed over many details, making it seem as though their swim to the chopper had been more relaxing than harrowing. But her grandmother wasn't so gullible. With a shrewd look at Sam, she said, "I hope you made him pay for those bruises on her face."

Sam gave a small nod, and she looked approving. But he knew the beating Oppenheimer had suffered at his hands was nothing compared to what he'd inflicted on Juliette, physically and emotionally. There wasn't a hell scorching enough to repay him for that.

"You must be relieved to be back home. If you'll excuse the two of us, we'll let you get unpacked." He ignored the frown Juliette tossed him, concentrating instead on Pauline's slow smile of comprehension.

"Of course. Why don't you take her out to the balcony? It's a lovely day."

Juliette preceded him to the French doors opening to the small terrace, pulse racing, not unhappy to play the rest of this scene out in private. Her response, however, was annoying. She was as jittery as a pickpocket in a roomful of police officers. Sam Tremaine was only a man, she reminded herself firmly, and no man had ever been allowed to shake her nerve. It was a matter of pride that her expression was schooled to an impassive demeanor when she faced him again. "Thank you for sparing my grandmother some of the details. They'd really serve no purpose, other than to upset her."

"I have a grandmother, remember?" he said mildly.

She relaxed enough to allow herself a small smile. "The one with the willow switches, yes."

He was watching her steadily, his green gaze seeing too much. "I wish you'd been spared some of those details."

Swallowing hard, she raised a shoulder. "It was my choice. One way or another, I had to have closure." In a flash she remembered her fear when it had looked as though Sam were going to pay for that choice. Remorse twisted through her, and more than a little guilt. "You called me single-minded once, and you were right. It's been so long since I considered anything other than revenge..." Her voice trailed off. One goal had guided her, directed her actions for ten years. And despite everything, she couldn't regret that. Not even now.

"Was it worth it?"

Her gaze flashed to his, but it wasn't judgment she found in his eyes, only acceptance. "I don't know." Her answer was as honest as she could manage.

"When it was over, I expected to feel…something."
She stopped, afraid to say more. The emptiness that
had been part of her for as long as she remembered
was still there. And the pain somehow was fresher.
But there was a deeper part of her, a fiercer part, that
had been mollified, somehow. It'd be a long time
before she could answer his question truthfully. All
she knew was that she couldn't have chosen another
way.

She cleared her throat. "I hadn't considered the
danger to you, though, and I am sorry for that. I'm
used to weighing my risks, but I had no right not to
consider yours."

Shrugging off her concern, he said, "You won't
have to weigh risks anymore, because I've arranged
for your retirement."

"You…" Words failed her for a moment as she
stared at him. It didn't take long, though, for annoyance to filter in. "*You've* arranged?"

One side of his mouth curled up in a way she
might have found beguiling if she weren't so irritated. "I destroyed the file on you, as I promised.
And I strong-armed Miles into leaving the name of
the thief we worked with out of his report." His
smile turned ruthless. "He was quite agreeable once
I found out that he hadn't been completely forthcoming with Headquarters when he'd sought approval for
the raid on the island."

"It sounds as if you've made it easier for me to
return to work, not more difficult," she pointed out,
purely for the sake of argument. "There's an impressive collection of netsukes going on auction at
Sotheby's next month. I've always had an appreciation for the unusual."

"We share that," he murmured, the light in his eyes giving his words a more personal meaning. "But you won't be planning any more thefts. What would be the point? The driving force behind it has been removed and if you need money..." He shrugged. "There's always the Moonfire necklace. I can't see you continuing to take risks when there's your grandmother to consider."

Despite the blatant manipulation of his argument, she glanced into the penthouse. He was right, and he knew it. Jeopardizing her future, and the remaining time she had with her grandmother, was no longer worth the gamble. She could recognize the truth in the realization while still mourning it.

"Hard to flush that need for adventure from your veins, though, isn't it?" Sam tucked his hands in his pockets and leaned against the balcony. "Some of us need those thrills the way others need oxygen. I can't quite see you settling down to a nine-to-five job selling cosmetics."

It was impossible to keep the look of horror from her face, even while she realized his eyes were laughing at her. "Credit me with a bit more imagination than that!"

"There's always another possibility. One that would allow you to continue what you do best, while removing the threat of imprisonment."

She was instantly wary, but couldn't prevent the immediate spark of interest that his words elicited. "What's that?"

"You could marry me. I could arrange for you to become a contract agent, with me as your handler. Or if that doesn't appeal to you, the agency is always looking for skilled members for their tech teams."

His explanation almost overshadowed his first sentence, *would have,* if she hadn't stopped listening the moment she'd heard it. "Marry you?" She didn't have to feign the panic in her voice. Her heart was quivering like a thoroughbred at the starting gate. "You don't want to marry me!"

He reached out, pulled her resisting form into his arms. "Amazingly, I do," he murmured, brushing his lips across her hair. "I knew I was in trouble the first time I saw you at the consulate party. And when you so obligingly threw yourself at me on the balcony—" He caught her hand in his before she could pinch him for that remark. "—I knew my objectivity was going to take a beating."

His confession was fascinating. Enthralling. She was torn by a need to hear more, and an equally strong desire to flee by leaping to the next balcony. She had nothing to offer him in return. She'd spent too many years suppressing all but one emotion. She wasn't sure she could even identify any others, much less experience them.

He had to have seen the alarm on her face. It didn't seem to deter him. His hands on her arms turned caressing. "I'd already come to terms with the fact that you'd shot my famed objectivity all to hell. But after I cut the power on the villa and slipped inside, saw Oppenheimer on top of you…" His grip tightened for a moment at the memory. "There's nothing I wouldn't have done to get you out of there safely. I love you, Juliette. I know that scares the hell out of you, but there it is."

She felt unbearably greedy, intolerably selfish. His words seeped into her soul and filled a portion of the void that had been there for so long. But she knew if wasn't fair to accept something that couldn't be returned.

Shaking her head, she said, "I can't...I don't feel the same way."

"I recognize it, even if you don't," he said, watching her intently. "I knew the moment I saw your face, when you thought I was going to surrender my weapon."

Her body shuddered with remembered terror at the memory. "I thought he'd kill you."

He skimmed his lips along her jawline. "And that would have bothered you?"

"Of course, you fool, I lo—" She stopped, shocked at the admission that had almost tumbled out of her mouth. Without conscious thought. Without her permission.

"Exactly." Satisfaction threaded the word as he worried her lobe with his teeth. "Now why don't you complete that sentence, leaving off the endearment."

Caution had filtered her earlier impulsivity. "I was concerned for you, yes. I..."

Her explanation was stemmed by the finger he placed against her lips. And the light in his eyes demanded honesty. "No rationalizations. Just listen to your heart."

Her heart. It hadn't been the most reliable organ of late. Surely that was why it was galloping so fiercely, making every pulse in her body throb like a wound.

She opened her mouth, closed it again. It was like the first time walking a tightrope without a net. The fear of falling, failing, was enough to choke her. Equally strong was the fear that something precious was on the verge of slipping from her grasp. "I think…that is…I may love you."

When he lifted his head, his lips were curved with genuine humor, deepening the sexy dent in his chin. "You can do better than that."

She felt like she was teetering on the edge of a towering precipice, with no guarantee of a soft landing. "I love you." He crushed her to him, and her arms went around his neck. She was giddy with the realization, with the freedom the words gave her, so she said them again. "I love you."

"There." There was a hint of purely masculine satisfaction in his voice. "That wasn't so difficult, was it?"

Juliette smiled up at him. "I have a feeling it'll get easier."

"And you won't miss the jobs? The excitement of holding something priceless in your hands?"

"No." It was a simple answer to give, a simple answer to mean. As she returned his kiss she was already certain that the most priceless thing she'd ever stolen was Sam's heart.

Epilogue

The wedding ceremony had gone beautifully, at least it had seemed so to Juliette. Sam's sister Ana had been a serene bride, contrasting with the broad-shouldered man who'd waited for her at the altar. Jones had appeared as ill at ease as a groom could be, until the instant he'd seen his fiancée. Then his face had transposed to an expression so fierce, so intensely personal, no one could mistake his devotion for the diminutive woman approaching him on her oldest brother's arm.

"You made a very handsome best man," she informed Sam afterward, as they strolled through the crowd of guests on the sprawling grounds of the Tremaine Louisiana home.

"Is that why you were undressing me with your eyes during the entire mass?" he inquired, nodding at an acquaintance.

"The male ego is a strange and wondrous thing."

It took real effort to keep the smile from her lips.
"More strange than wondrous, actually."

His arm slipped around her waist. "Be good or I'll
sit you down next to my grandmother and let her
grill you about your past. And you better have an
answer ready for when she questions you about your
intentions of making an honest man of me. She's
never said it out loud, but I always figured I was her
favorite."

Juliette looked around, located his grandmother
where she was sitting and watching the festivities.
Waving to her, she said, "Actually, she's already
warned me about you. Said you were slick and
charming and not to be trusted."

He snatched a quick kiss. "She's an excellent
judge of character."

"I could have told you the same thing," another
voice put in. Recognizing it, she turned, found Cade
Tremaine on her other side. There was more than a
flavor of the South in his speech. It reminded Juliette
of a slow walk along a lazy river. But there was
nothing quite so harmless about his hard jaw, or
about the set of his mouth. Or his smile that couldn't
quite banish the ghosts in his eyes.

Seeing his brother, Sam immediately sobered.
"What's this I hear about you returning to work next
week?"

Cade reached out and slapped a passing guest on
the shoulder. "Your hearing was always good."

"You could give the healing more time." Sam
shrugged under his brother's narrowed gaze. "Not
that I care much, but grandma worries. Ever since
you fell off that garage roof—"

"You pushed me off that roof."

''—I've felt a certain interest in your well-being,'' Sam continued, ignoring his brother's interruption. ''Another week isn't going to make a difference, is it?''

Mentally, Juliette agreed. There was still a pallor to Cade's skin, and a gauntness to his frame. But there was no mistaking the determination in his quiet voice. ''I've got three holes in my chest, and my partner is dead. The trail for our shooter is going cold. So, yeah, I'd say another week would make a difference.'' He walked off, leaving Sam to frown after him. But when he would have followed his younger brother, Juliette laid her hand on his arm to stop him.

''Something tells me he doesn't like to be told what to do any more than you.''

''He isn't thinking clearly.''

''Maybe not. But it's his decision to make.'' She could empathize with Cade's need for action, even while she sympathized with his brother's worry for him.

Sam released a breath. Reaching for her hand, he pressed a kiss to the palm. ''You're very wise.''

''I'll remind you of that the next time we have an argument.''

''I don't doubt it.'' Smiling, he lowered her hand to play with her bare fingers. ''We still need to find you a ring.''

''I could pick something up.'' The innocence in her suggestion didn't fool him.

''When my ring goes on your finger it will be one we acquire the old-fashioned way. By paying for it.''

''Spoilsport.'' The regret tinging her words wasn't totally feigned. But it was more than diffused by the

warm glow of heat that spread through her at the
thought of wearing Sam's ring. They'd have to pick
out an ageless style. She planned to be wearing it for
the next seventy or eighty years.

* * * * *

*Be sure to look for the next book
in* THE TREMAINE TRADITION *miniseries,
TRUTH OR LIES, featuring Cade,
in August 2003!*

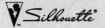

If you enjoyed what you just read,
then we've got an offer you can't resist!

Take 2 bestselling
love stories FREE!

Plus get a FREE surprise gift!

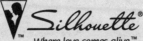

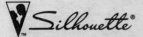
COMING NEXT MONTH

SIMCNM0503